A P

WHY AR

ERIC WHITE

JASON PORTER was born and raised in southeastern Michigan. He is, or has been, an English teacher, customer support representative, landlord, traveling musician, and the overnight editor for Yahoo! News and the *New York Times*. Currently, he writes fiction. *Why Are You So Sad?* is his first novel.

Praise for *Why Are You So Sad?*

"*Why Are You So Sad?* is wry, sardonic, very smart, and hilariously critical of the futility and general mediocrity of life in America as we know it."

—Patrick McGrath, author of *Asylum* and *Constance*

"*Why Are You So Sad?*: Why are you so funny, so wry, so true, so compelling? Jason Porter's lovely book is perfect and wondrous, a masterfully crafted story of modernity. I ate it whole."

—Jennifer Traig, author of memoirs *Devil in the Details: Scenes from an Obsessive Girlhood* and *Well Enough Alone: A Cultural History of My Hypochondria*

"Existential despair has never been so funny. *Why Are You So Sad?* is a great American comedy, perfectly tuned to this ridiculous age. Jason Porter is a Kafka with better jokes."

—Larry Doyle, author of *I Love You, Beth Cooper*

"*Why Are You So Sad?* is a precisely calibrated comedy pitched halfway between a laugh and a sob. Beautifully written, philosophically unsound, and funny."

—Sara Levine, author of *Treasure Island!!!*

"Porter starts with a loaded question and takes aim at our compromises and deferred dreams, at our unquestioned normalcy—and he hits us where we live. But this is Camus crossed with Stanley Elkin, a brilliant book that's as funny as it is wise."

—Jeffrey Rotter, author of *The Unknown Knowns*

JASON PORTER

WHY ARE YOU SO SAD?

A Novel

A PLUME BOOK

PLUME
Published by the Penguin Group
Penguin Group (USA) LLC
375 Hudson Street
New York, New York 10014

USA | Canada | UK | Ireland | Australia | New Zealand | India | South Africa | China
penguin.com
A Penguin Random House Company

First published by Plume, a member of Penguin Group (USA) LLC, 2014

Copyright © 2014 by Jason Porter

 REGISTERED TRADEMARK—MARCA REGISTRADA

ISBN 978-0-14-218058-7

Printed in the United States of America
10 9 8 7 6 5 4 3 2 1

Set in Palatino LT Std

For Trucker, Petey, and Shelly

The present generation, wearied by its chimer-
ical efforts, relapses into complete indolence. Its
condition is that of a man who has only fallen
asleep towards morning: first of all come great
dreams, then a feeling of laziness, and finally a
witty or clever excuse for remaining in bed.

—SØREN KIERKEGAARD

PART ONE

SHORT ANSWER

PART ONE

I was in my bed when the thought came to me: Have we all sunken into a species-wide bout of clinical depression? A severe, but subtle, despondency, germinating in every single one of us. The thought hit me. Smacked me as true. Its flawless pitch rang on and on, adhering to my consciousness like shit on shoe.

I was on my back. My hands making a tent on my sternum. I was staring at the ceiling fan spinning above, its body wobbling gently in reaction to its rotating blades. It was a sort of meditation, focusing on the blades; an attempt to quiet my senses and fall into sleep. As if the thought were not distracting enough, a car alarm went off outside. A squawking robotic bird with Tourette's syndrome. But I pressed on. Still committed to easing my mind, I endeavored to appreciate the beauty of the silence that existed between the beeps and screams of my neighbor's BMW. It was a nearly impossible task, but in those spaces I did find something. I found the calls of the dead. I found the dinosaurs. They said, *It started like this for us too. We were down. Nobody noticed because it was gradual. It snuck in like fog. We were moody and sluggish and complacent, and we were too busy eating things to take notice.*

In time the car alarm relented. I stared with even greater focus at the ceiling fan. I could hear the buzz of the lighting element in the reading lamp. I was aware of every hair on my body. I itched. I knew that at the very least, I was depressed. I wondered if the depression had always been there. It was not unlike listening to the song "American Pie." You reach a point in the song when you ask yourself, "Have I always been listening to this song?" To answer yes defies rationality, but to answer no discredits your experiential reality.

I reconfigured. I fluffed the pillows. I got fetal. Closing my eyes, focusing inward, I tried to call up something cheerful that might set my thoughts on a hopeful course—a giggling infant, the toss of a wedding bouquet, a grandfather happy to receive a call from his grandson—but all I could think of were third-world viruses that sold newspapers and dissolved brains. I quickly composed a mental catalog of friends, colleagues, former roommates, elderly neighbors, and the anonymous faces who sell me gasoline, deliver my mail, and fill my prescriptions; I uncovered alcoholics, overwhelmed parents, hoarders, diet addicts, news junkies, tabloid gobblers, sexless marriages, teenage diabetics, cell phone dependents, and uninsured back pains resulting from unresolved childhood rage.

I rolled over to get my wife's opinion. She was lost in a

gigantic children's novel. Her brown eyes, even bigger behind glasses, were scanning the pages left to right. In her
glasses I could see the whole room reflected. I could see the
white curtains we bought at a bargain through my employee discount, the matching dressers purchased through
the same discount, and a fern that wasn't thriving. I took
turns looking at her through one eye while the other was
closed, toggling back and forth. From both perspectives
she didn't seem to notice I was staring at her.

I said, "Brenda, is it me or is every single person we
know depressed?"

She let out a dramatic sigh and slowly closed her book.
She didn't want to leave the story. As she turned to look at
me she spilled a little bourbon. It's a habit of hers. It drib-
bled down her chin and onto her nightgown. She kissed
me on the forehead like she was putting a stamp on a letter,
and said, "You are." And then as she turned off her light
and shifted onto her side, facing away from me, she said,
"I'm not."

She wasn't one to dress things up. I let what she said
settle, but it did nothing to calm my anxieties. I inched over
and held her. She didn't feel dead. Nor did she feel awake.
I then reached past her, taking the bourbon from her nightstand, almost knocking over her alarm clock. Like a baby
bird being fed by its mother, I held the glass over my mouth
for every last drop, enjoying the harsh warmth in my throat
and chest.

The bourbon made no difference. I stared at the ceiling
fan for hours.

Are you single?

No, I am married to Brenda Champs, for-
merly Brenda Brynschzchvsksy. She took
my name, Champs, not out of some nod to
tradition, but because she hated having a
name nobody could ever pronounce, including her new husband, me. It certainly
wasn't for the children, because we don't
have any.

The following morning I found myself no less preoccupied. I was driving to work. My car stereo had been stolen the previous week. I could hear my thoughts too clearly: That man driving that car is sick. That other man driving that other car is sick. I am sick. We are all sick. Something is in the water. It is in the soil. We are all symptoms of a grieving planet.

I was coming up on the backup to the General Eisenhower Bridge. We were all merging to pay the toll. Traffic choked on itself here without fail. Red brake lights flickered. Drivers were greedy about their lanes. Their despair and emptiness reached out to me through the glass and steel and molded plastic. I could feel myself in each car. I was for a moment each of these people. I felt it all. And it was their breath mints that pushed me over the edge.

I realize that sounds a little crazy. But hear me out. I heard their talk radio: awful. I chewed on their fingernails: mindless. I sipped on their lukewarm coffee while gazing at their reflections in the rearview mirror: hateful. I felt the way they dreamed about what might happen next in their lives: lonely, depressing, barely imaginative. But nothing was worse than the breath mints. I carefully imagined breaking them down with my tongue. Pressing them into the roof of my mouth. It tipped the scales. It was revolting. They tasted as if the chemists who design all of our commercial food additives had developed a purely artificial flavor that was in itself the absence of flavor. They were minty, sure, but in such an intentionally absent way. Hardened on the edges by the sharp chemical nontaste of erased calories. It was absolutely horrid. The fact that all these people could suck on these mints, driving along in a limping herd, actively not tasting things—it overwhelmed me. Completely. This was disease. Rot. Evolutionary peril. My empathic sensors, or whatever the hell they were, were overheating. Watching the stuttering cars, and all the miserable, unsuspecting people trapped inside of them, it became obvious that I needed to either confirm or disprove my suspicion. I needed to get some irrefutable science behind this. Otherwise it risked carrying on in my mind like a phantom odor: *What is that smell? Is something burning? Maybe I am only imagining that something is burning? Am I imagining that something is burning? Am I burning?*

What I needed was an emotional Geiger counter that could objectively measure other people for sadness. I looked at the woman in the car next to me. She was applying makeup during the stops, opening and closing her mouth like a feeding fish, staring at her red lips in the rearview mirror. I imagined holding the Geiger counter to her forehead. I would ask her a question about her children. Were they an accident? What dreams did they make impossible? She would say, "They are the best thing I ever did," and the readout would expose her lie with a pixelated frown.

Starting up the bridge, I looked down at the water. It was the bottom of the bay, where the filth comes to die. Twigs and feathers and candy wrappers were suspended in a gray foam that was undulating along the shoreline. Ahead of me, the sun, charcoal orange and hazy, was beautiful like a bruise. It was hot, and it smogged down on me past housing projects and strip malls and strip clubs and furniture marts, into a shifting desert of corporate parks. About a mile short of our offices, I passed a billboard for a vacation resort that said "Put Your Dreams to the Test." The words were paired with a picture of a doctor in a Hawaiian T-shirt holding a stethoscope up to a piña colada. It was the stupidest thing I had ever seen. I couldn't make any sense of it, but the word *test* stayed with me. A test. An exam. A questioning.

Which led me to my decisive course of action: I would take a random sampling at work. All the necessary data was waiting for me in the office. It was too simple. The people there are compliant. They do as they are told, like sheep waiting for paychecks. Corralled over to meetings that serve no purpose. Filling out forms they never hear about again. Sitting in on career-development workshops with box lunches and guest speakers who had just flown in from the middle of the country. It was a natural fixture within the terrain, jumping through unnecessary hoops. If I were to ask a few personal questions, assuming the formatting was authoritatively insipid, nobody would be the wiser. That was the plan. I would compose a survey, deftly crafted to root out the true feelings of those around me. If the sampling supported my fear—the gradual but certain emotional demise of the world's population—then, well, I didn't know. I would have to do something. Reprioritize my life. Circle the wagons. Notify the authorities. Conduct more focused research. I would give the epidemic my full attention. This might not be good for my career. I would have to work part-time or take a leave of absence. There would be definite and irreversible consequences. Brenda would not be happy, but who was?

I turned into the parking lot next to the sign for our offices that read "LokiLoki: Everyday Living Is Getting Better Every Day," and found a space by a newly planted tree. The tree still had a tag on it. It was the shadiest spot available.

In the cramped discomfort of my Korean hatchback, I thought up questions that would trigger heartfelt responses from my colleagues. I found an empty brown bag under the passenger seat and scribbled down the following:

—*Are you single?*
—*Are you having an affair?*
—*Why are you so sad?*
—*When was the last time you felt happy?*
—*Was it a true, pure happy or a relative happy?*

The last question edged up against a greasy stain left by a pastry that was no longer in the bag. It looked like the word *happy* was going to enter a dark brown hole, as if the entire sentence was a train about to funnel into the side of a mountain. I thought briefly of caves. I imagined an afternoon stroll in the woods leading me to a hillside cavern, and curiosity drawing me in. I would lean against a wall at the very edge of where the outside light was lost to the world's dark interior. I would pause, rub my eyes, adjust to the lack of light, and without realizing it find myself talking to a company of bats. Sharing ideas. Learning about each other's worlds. It turns out they don't particularly miss seeing things. I would say, "I think it is precisely because I see things that I trip over them." The bats would laugh and fly directly at me and then around me and out into the evening.

I began to perspire. The sun, even through the haze, was stifling. The car was becoming a hot house.

I wrote more questions:

—*Are you who you want to be?*
—*Would you prefer to be someone else?*
—*Are you similar to the "you" you thought you would become when as a child you imagined your future self?*
—*Is today worse than yesterday?*
—*If you were a day of the week, would you be Monday or Wednesday?*
—*What does it feel like to get out of bed in the morning?*

A car pulled in next to me. I grabbed for my cell phone and pretended to be in the middle of a conversation: "No, no, no . . . That's putting it mildly . . . Of course not . . . Yes, yes, yes . . . You tell me . . . Well, that takes the cake . . . Absolutely not . . . Are you deaf? . . . That is not acceptable."

It was Bob Grasston. We started at LokiLoki on the same day more than a decade ago. I am a Senior Pictographer, North American Division. I draw the instructional diagrams for the assembly manuals. I can't remember what Bob does, exactly—something involving charts and projections—but I see him every year when they call us in for flu shots. We have consecutive employee numbers.

He was in a cobalt blue sports car that didn't suit him. It was too sleek. Too lecherous. It beeped as he waved his keychain, commanding the car to lock from a distance of several feet. I gave him a nod while I said, "You better believe I mean it," to my phone. He paused, maybe thinking I would get out and walk with him, but then he went on down the footpath toward the Business Development Tower. He was carrying a briefcase and a gym bag. The way his belt cinched his dress shirt into his slacks made him look doughy, like a pork bun with a goatee.

I did some quick calculations:

—*Do you realize you have on average another 11,000 to 18,250 mornings of looking in the mirror and wondering if people will find you attractive?*
—*Do you think people will remember you after you die?*
—*For how long after you die?*

I paused and looked up for more inspiration. The windshield was covered in dead insects. I wondered what it must feel like to have a speeding plane of shatterproof glass catapulting your exoskeleton into flatness.

—*Do you believe in God?*
—*Do you believe in life after death?*
—*Do you believe in life after God?*
—*Do you hear voices?*
—*Are you for the chemical elimination of all things painful?*
—*Do you think we need more sports?*

It was a good survey.

If you were a day of the week, would you be Monday or Wednesday?

I would be a Wednesday, but in a week that went Wednesday, Wednesday, Wednesday, Wednesday, Wednesday, Wednesday, Wednesday, and repeat.

Every aspect of our workspace was decorated in strict reverence to LokiLoki's official colors: electric salmon and evergreen. Under the buzz of fluorescent lighting the colors could at times look radioactive. Walking through the maze of shimmering office partitions was like getting lost in a durably carpeted cornfield. Stalks of filing cabinets and impermanent desk dividers shot up taller than basketball players. Passing each row revealed another identical row, and the rows extended in every direction. I kept my bearings by looking for environmental markers within the cubicles. To get to my desk from the east entrance, I turned right at the puppy calendar, right again at the cross-eyed honor student, followed by a left at the fat black goldfish with the disfigured dorsal fin.

As a defense against the miserable fabric that covered the walls of my cubicle, I had posted as many photographs as I could find. Anything that might protect me from the obscene company pink. An amateur football player with turf caked on his helmet was crying in defeat. A bull with blood gushing out of its side was chasing after a matador. A frozen beach was littered with plastic bottles and dead seagulls. Some were photos I had taken. Others were cut out from magazines or the newspaper. One of my favorites, of a child soldier, stared down from above my monitor. He was pointing an automatic weapon at me. According to the magazine article about him, he was hardened by cheap drugs forced on him by his captors and from an adolescence that consisted of firing on villagers from the back of a pickup.

I wondered how he would answer my survey.

—*I am single.*
—*I am too young to have an affair.*
—*What does "future self" mean?*
—*I believe in death after death after death.*
—*I like sports. We play soccer, but then somebody shoots at the ball with a gun because they lost, and I want to cry but am afraid that if they see me cry I will get shot or left behind.*
—*I am sad because my father has been replaced by a teenager in sunglasses. And this same teenager raped my mother before killing her, and now my choice is to be his friend or to have no friends at all.*
—*Today is worse than yesterday.*

I felt that too. Worse than yesterday. I set to work on typing up the survey. I was in the middle of trying to de-

cide which font would be the most therapeutic when
Brenda called.

"How are you feeling?"

"Why?"

"I'm your wife. I can ask these questions."

"I don't know."

"Well, that's an improvement."

"Okay, I guess I feel like a robot that was programmed
to believe it was a little boy, but that just cut itself and to its
dismay discovers it can't bleed."

"What the fuck does that mean?"

"I don't know what the fuck it means. What about
you? How are *you* feeling?"

"You shouldn't swear at work."

I could hear people in the background at her work typing and talking business. Brenda works in marketing. She
is Senior Sloganeer. She has done very well. She ascended
quickly because she scares the shit out of people. I can't say
exactly when this started. There may have been a make-
over in there. Aggressive outfits and high-tech weekly
planners suddenly appeared as if they had always been a
part of her life. Maybe some of it was accidentally added to
her personality when she got hypnosis to help her quit
smoking. Or it might have happened around the time she
became concerned with something she referred to as her
"core."

"I saw a man that looked like your father panhandling
under the President Truman Overpass on the way to
work," she said. "I just thought I would tell you."

"Oh."

"What are you working on?"

"Something important."

"Don't get fired."

I tried to hang up first, but she beat me to it.

I added a few more questions:

—Have you ever fallen in love?

—If yes, were you surprised that it, like all other things,
*   faded over time?*

—Would you equate this to the way that gum loses its
*   flavor, or more to the way all food loses its heat?*

I looked over the questions, checking for spelling er-
rors. I read them aloud, but very quietly, to myself, to make
sure they made sense. I decided on a title that I hoped
would lend an air of institutional credibility—"Emotional
Well-Being Self-Appraisal"—but it still wasn't enough. After a little internal brainstorming I added: "Please complete
forms within forty-eight hours and return to the desk of
Raymond Champs, Senior Pictographer, Row 8, Pod D
(Customer Acclaim, Employee Regard, Product Elucida-
tion, Quantity Assurance, and Technical Support). All information will be treated as confidential." I read it back to
myself several times. Would I believe it was an official document had I not written it? Would I get caught? Was this a
good idea? I looked up at the child soldier's photo, and his
hardened child eyes seemed to say, *How the fuck should I*
know?, while also saying, *Why the fuck should I care?* He

made a compelling argument holding that automatic weapon. I sent the document to print at the laser printer over on the south wing. Fifty copies.

Along the narrow corridor to the laser printer, the wall to my left was real. Real drywall painted a forest green, with windows looking into empty conference rooms. On my right was a series of three-quarter walls that could be reconfigured at the whim of a middle manager. As I walked past, I was able to steal glances in; my colleagues were all tucked into their stations like sailors in their bunks. They all shared a universal slump, their backs to me, their heads bending in toward the glow of their screens. Their hearts had slowed down. They were barely breathing. Soft, inert bodies with all motion isolated to one little hand clicking on one little mouse. That was their only motion, and it was incessant. They reminded me of hamsters sucking on water bottles, but they were clicking and clicking and clicking instead of sucking and sucking and sucking.

Nora Pepperdine was at the printer talking to Charlie Danglish. They were laughing. I didn't like the way he leaned in toward her. He was married. He wasn't young, but he was still athletic and attractive enough to sell things. He had broken the record for most hideaway beds sold in a year, a record he had set himself the previous year. His sales successes catapulted him to the head of the Customer Acclaim department. People, but not all people, tended to like him. He had a disarming smile. He spent a lot of money on dress shoes.

Nora was the object of all of our fantasies. No one

needed to confirm this. It was in all of the male eyes, and
many female eyes too, whenever she stood up to offer a
little pep at one of the all-hands meetings. She had the perk
of an Olympic athlete. I hated the perk, but sometimes I
imagined myself pressed up against it, asphyxiating myself in the high altitudes of her exuberance.

They were reading my survey. The fresh stack had
been waiting at the printer unprotected. That was why
they were laughing. Nora's sparkling curls were laughing
along with her, and Charlie was still leaning in. He put an
arm on her shoulder, as if she might need some support
while she laughed. In his laughing mouth were perfect
white teeth. I looked at his perfect teeth and imagined the
skeleton beneath the salesman flesh.

"I see you have the survey everyone is talking about?"
I said it cool. I was focused. This was important.

"Raymond," Nora said, though I had told her so many
times she was welcome to call me Ray. "What do you know
about this? It's very unusual."

"How does it make you feel to read it?" I asked.

They looked as if they didn't see the connection between reading a survey on feelings and having feelings.

"All I know is I heard that everybody is meant to take
it," I said. "It's part of our biquarterly assessments, not as
a measure of our performance but merely as an opportu-
nity to check in and make sure we are all doing fine, emo-
tionally that is." It was a fib, fluttering out of my mouth
like a moth in search of light. I added, hoping it might
help convince them, "They don't want us to feel any of

this low, quiet crushing that some suspect might be going around."

Charlie's hand awkwardly remained on Nora's shoulder for a moment, until it looked out of place. He must have sensed this. He slowly retracted it and put it in his pocket, and when that wasn't right he crossed his arms against his chest. They both looked at me, uncertain.

"But I could be wrong," I said. "All I know is that I heard Jerry Samberson really wants us to take this seriously, put some thought into it, and open up as much as possible."

Jerry was our boss. People joked that he was born in the company nursery, though I've also never heard it refuted. I don't think I have ever seen him leave the campus. He was the one who thought we should call it a "campus."

I stared at Nora a little too long after I had said all of this. I got lost in her curls. They were like ribbons coaxed into coils by master gift wrappers.

I sensed Charlie staring at me staring at her.

I broke the silence. "Do you mind distributing the survey along your aisles? I am sure Jerry will appreciate it. I have to get back to diagrams for the new reversible book closet they are pushing for the holidays." I turned away before they could answer.

I worked on some drawings to get my mind off of the survey. I was at it for over an hour. I must have thrown away five or six drafts. The man I was trying to draw, the man I always draw, Mr. CustomMirth®, wasn't his usual self under my distracted hand. His potato-shaped body was not whimsical enough. It was agitated and shaky. Impatient. His balloon nose was edging perilously on the brink of ethnic. I was unable to work. All I could think about were the answers that would come back to me. And then all I could think about was how exactly I might go about alerting the world to its own infection. Who would listen to me? How could I continue to work while sending out the distress calls? If I wasn't working, how would I pay for a full-page ad in a major periodical?

I heard a throat clear and smelled the thaw of company bagels. Don Ables had entered my cube. Don worked a few cubes down, where he worked harder than anybody else. He was a soft man with milky flesh and hair that stained pillowcases. He lived with his sister. One of them took care of the other. Nobody had met the sister. There was a terrible photo of her on his desk that we all tried not to stare at. The light in the photo was all wrong. Her face was mostly shadow. You couldn't tell how many eyebrows she had.

"Hello, Don."

He looked unsettled.

To break the silence, I said, "In the science-fiction movies you watch, what do the townspeople do when they discover something monstrous from beyond is breeding in the municipality's waste treatment plant?"

"Is this some kind of cruel joke?" He was holding the survey. His small gray eyes looked pinched.

"I'm not sure what you are talking about," I said. I

knew exactly what he was talking about and was encouraged by his distress.

"Nora came into my cube and put this on my desk," he said. The words came from deep within his chest. His belly quivered. "At least four of these questions are explicitly targeted at me."

I had never seen Don so upset. Until that moment he had struck me as somebody who, however miserable, felt a certain sense of relief because he would never have to attend high school again. His presence no longer evacuated lunch tables.

"She said that you were collecting them. I don't understand what this is about."

"I don't either, Don."

"I don't like it."

For a split second I betrayed myself with the slightest smile, because I was pleased that my questions were uncovering these feelings in Don, but I quickly transitioned to a sympathetic nod, which I hoped masked any trace of authorship. He placed the survey facedown in the workspace opposite my computer. I heard his shoes squeak as he walked back to his cube. I thought I could hear his office chair react to his weight. I listened for his tears, or cries, or perhaps a distraught call to his sister. Then I simply began to listen. People coughed. Throats were cleared. Fingers typed. There was whispering through walls. The north entrance beeped as somebody either entered or exited. The lights above hummed in all their institutional cheapness. Deep within the humming I thought I heard a foghorn half a continent away. Everything I thought I heard began to sound muffled by mist. Beyond the horn I heard my mother telling me it was too dark outside to play. Yelling at me from the front porch of our old house, the yellow one with the ivy growing up the sides. Yelling up and down, left and right, because it was quickly dark, and in shadows I could be anywhere and anything; I could be behind the parked car, I could be hiding in a shed, I could be up in a tree. She said, as if talking down a wild cat, "Come in and watch *Love Boat*."

Would you prefer to be someone else?

I am not sure that I am even me anymore.
To be good at my job, I must eliminate
feeling, surprise, and abstract thought
from the creative process. It's like being told to kiss a beautiful woman but
that you must under no circumstances let
it arouse you. When you start the job,
you tell yourself it is merely a matter
of compartmentalizing these things. You
put them in a drawer, somewhere inside
of you—the passion, the inner thoughts
that drive you and inspire you, the
dreams that are too pure to decipher,
that tell you to paint a sky yellow, or
to draw a woman laughing in the rain
with hair on fire, or any other crazy
thing that is beautiful because it barely
makes sense. You tuck these parts of
yourself away for safekeeping, and years
later, when you are on vacation, on maybe
the third day of the vacation, when you
have exhausted all of the entertainment
features of the resort and you find you
have nothing else to do, you open up the
drawer, just to check in on those organs
of emotion you have stored away, and you
find they have shrunken and dried out
like an old dead beetle.

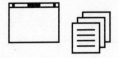

I drew up an official-looking sign with "Surveys" written on it and an arrow that pointed to a wire basket I had stolen from the supply cabinet. In the basket I placed a large manila envelope upon which I had written "Confidential." I put Don's survey in there. I wanted to read it desperately, but I didn't want to get caught reading it. Somebody passing by or dropping in with a question could catch me in the act. People needed to believe this was coming from the top.

The phone rang. "Are you still working on something 'important'?"

"Hi, Brenda."

"You didn't tell anybody about the robot, did you?"

"What?"

"The robot that doesn't bleed, or whatever that gibberish was earlier."

"Are you starting to feel that way too?"

"I often feel like a machine. It's called getting shit done."

I wrote this down on a pad of paper. She might be a lost cause.

"But listen, Ray, you didn't tell people at work that, did you? That you are a boy robot? Don't start talking like that at work. You can say that nonsense to me, because we have a legally binding agreement that I won't leave you in sickness or health. But they'll dump your ass faster than microwave popcorn if you start talking like that."

"I haven't had a meaningful conversation with anybody here in over ten years."

"Good. We recently fired somebody for saying he believed the earth has a consciousness."

"What?"

"Exactly. Right in the middle of a team-building breakfast. He was packing his things before lunch."

"I have to get back to work."

"That's the spirit." She hung up.

More surveys trickled in while I worked on a drawing for our new whisper mop. I was trying to give the mop a face. The face was to look up and wink at Mr. Custom-Mirth®, who was mopping up a spill. I was pleased with the face on the mop. It was playful and compliant. The spill, however, looked too much like something regurgitated, a hearty stew come back from the digested. I crumpled up the drawing and stared blankly at my computer.

I needed a break. I peeked out into the aisle, and when I was sure nobody could see me I grabbed a completed survey from the envelope and snuck off to the company gym.

The gym was all mirrors. A kaleidoscope of white

metal fitness machines. I grabbed a communal magazine stacked next to a chain of stationary bicycles. I was the only exerciser. I could see at least twelve of my selves: pale limbs, flushed cheeks, flimsy bodies.

Concealed in last September's issue of *Man Health*, I took a look at Van Wilson's self-appraisal. Van was a nepotism case. His mother was best friends with Jerry Samberson's mother. Van wrote:

```
I think we should have more sports. I
think if a guy is really good at some
sports, like riflery, then he should get
credit at work and at home, because it
shows he can focus and really make some-
thing happen.
```

It made me dizzy to run and read at the same time. I slowed the treadmill to a brisk walk, climbing a hill ranked level three. I noticed in the reflections that my hair in the back was melting away into a circle of unprotected scalp. These mirrors defied my active hair-loss denial.

I read more:

```
I am totally a Monday, because Sunday,
when it isn't football season, I work
on things and play virtual golf and
kind of get in touch with stuff, and
I'll call an old buddy and drive my car
around and sometimes walk around the
mall, just kind of getting to know my
```

thoughts and checking out sales and
magazines, and then I go to a movie or
maybe catch a buffet somewhere. So I am
more or less Sunday—that is my day. I
am Sunday. But since that isn't a
choice, I figure Monday is closer to
Sunday than Wednesday, unless you say
that the week starts with Monday and
you can't get to Sunday until you have
gone through Wednesday, but I don't
think that's what you mean by this question. I see the week as more of a wheel,
and that is why I am closer to Monday
than Wednesday. I am a Monday.

Van was probably in denial. That was okay. I should
have expected this. A likely symptom of the epidemic.

The men's locker room was empty. It smelled like
bleach and dirty socks. Sports-themed music was coming
out of tiny round holes in the carpeted ceiling. I decided to
take a sauna. It is the one place in all of the buildings that
isn't air-conditioned.

I sat on the top bench, wearing my towel like a skirt. I
ladled water on the rocks. They hissed. I sat and wished
that I could travel back in time and get a representative
sample of depressed people through the ages. My research
could benefit from some graphs. I wanted to chart the
course of humanity's collective spirit over time. The Middle Ages might have been a low. That could be good news.
This might be cyclical, like sunspots or El Niño.

I was starting to perspire.

Bob Grasston came in, looking even more like a steamed dumpling wearing nothing but a white towel.

"Bob."

"Raymond."

A light moss of hair grew on his shoulders. He was holding a folder of papers.

"What are you working on?"

"I'm charting quarterly sales growth and weighing it against personnel costs."

"Sounds pointy," I said. It was all I could offer.

He was one level below me. He had a cell phone clipped to his towel. I thought I saw the edge of one of the surveys peeking out from under the sheets of business data in the folder.

I was still holding Van's survey, brazenly, now unprotected by the magazine I had left back with the bicycles. I rolled Van up into the shape of a telescope and wiped sweat from my brow. I was at the threshold of what I can endure in the sauna, but I was curious to see if Bob was going to fill out his survey.

I stared at his shoulders in awkward silence. We sweat. I became impatient.

"Is that the emotional well-being survey you have there?" I asked, and only then did it occur to me that Bob shouldn't have had one of the surveys. He was in a different organizational pod. He worked in a different building.

"It is."

I could feel a trickle down my back. Perspiration

bloomed out of my pores. My face felt like it looked like a tomato.

"I see you have a survey too." He gestured toward Van's survey.

"I figure it must be important."

Bob's flesh was heating up. The hair follicles on his arms were red and irritated. His forearms looked like plucked drumsticks. My mind drifted briefly to cannibalism. I imagined us surviving a plane crash together, or being the only two to remain after a global pandemic. Could I build a fire without matches? Could I clean out his entrails? Would I know how? Would hot sauce be available?

"Could I take a look at your survey?" he asked.

This was a dilemma. I wanted to see his survey. I could have suggested we swap, but I wasn't holding my own.

"It's kind of personal," I said.

He nodded in agreement and poured some more water on the rocks. I could taste salt on my lips.

"Does anybody know where this is coming from?" he asked.

"I assumed it was coming from the top."

"I see."

"It seems like a great idea, though."

"It does?" Bob said.

My arms were a puddled street after a storm.

"Well, I can see how unhappiness might sneak up on people, or collectively on a staff, or a company, or a country, or on a species. And we are busy. We are occupied with our work. We have an obligation to the home office in Iceland. We have an obligation to Georg Loki—may he rest in peace—who started making furniture for everyday lives fifty years ago, trying to fill his time during the endless nights of winter." I was beginning to sound like the video that Human Resources played during the orientation training for new employees. I thought sounding like the video would appeal to Bob's corporate patriotism. "Because we are working and living our everyday lives, maybe we don't realize that we're all a little under the weather, on an emotional level. At least, that is what I'm guessing they are after with this."

"Interesting." He nodded and wrote something down, shielding it from my view, then nodded again.

I felt my heart beating back where my earlobes attach to my head. He was waiting for me to say more.

"Well, I think this turkey is just about cooked," I said. It was his meaty arms that had me thinking of poultry. I hoped he wasn't aware of the association. "I better get a move on," I said. "I have to draw up the instructions for the new party sofa."

I left Bob to roast.

The stack of surveys on my desk had not grown substantially. I tried looking on the bright side: People were giving this thought, taking stock, considering their true feelings. It might take a while. I needed to be patient. It was a good survey.

What does it feel like to get out of bed in the morning?

It feels like pulling a sequoia out of the earth with your bare hands.

It is my very clear understanding that dreams, like apartment buildings, are composed of many floors and rooms. I was in the third-floor alcove of an Edwardian manor, curled up in a nest of Turkish pillows, thumb in my mouth, getting my belly rubbed by a talking panda bear, when news from the first-floor radio cracked the patina. Political scandals, flash floods, and celebrity drug busts rose up like smoke, bleeding into paradise and drowning out the gentle affirmations of my soft-pawed friend.

Golden warmth dissolved into earthly bedroom. I opened my eyes and spied a black dress sock hanging out of our overstuffed laundry hamper.

Waking up was like reversing a burial; I was a Cartesian brain alive in a coffin, aware of my own thoughts and the requirements of the living, but with no will to rise and proceed with my life. If it weren't for my bladder, I might never have gotten up. I had to pee, therefore I was.

Downstairs, Brenda was at the kitchen table, humming

something that wasn't on the radio, eating cereal, reading the paper, making lists. Her hair and face were already in place. She was a morning person. It didn't matter that she drank the night before. You could run her over with a tractor and the next morning she would be up with the birds, laying out breakfast options, paying bills, alphabetizing the spices.

Milk and cereal had been left out on the kitchen counter. Everything was fortified. I joined her at the table, looking into my bowl of cereal, preparing to eat it. All the cereal rings looked like clones of each other. They were all the same. I longed for something uglier and less Space Age. A spotting banana or the uneven terrain of breakfast sausage.

I heard a newscaster talk about congressional hearings on the homeless. There was a proposal to use them for medical research. Another proposal to farm their organs. "Let's give these people a purpose," a Southern politician was heard saying on the Senate floor.

Brenda held a spoonful of cereal by her mouth, waiting until she had finished digesting an important point in one of the editorials before finally rewarding herself with the oat rings. She moved on to another section of the paper, scooped up more cereal, and chuckled at a cartoon.

"Do you think it is strange that we now gladly eat things that are so uniform?" I asked my wife. "Don't you think we take too much comfort in the unnatural?"

"There is a funny piece about body bags in the Living section," she said. Her jaw was making those noises while she chewed: another postmatrimonial discovery. She swal-

lowed and said, "I filled out this little joke of yours," passing the survey across the table like it was some dirty thing
she had found on the street.

"Oh," I said. I must have left a copy out on the table. A
mistake. She was likely to dismiss my concerns. To dis-
courage my project. To threaten me with practicalities.

"Oh?" She said it like a stern teacher.

"Maybe I got carried away."

She started saying other things, a lot of things, but I
couldn't hear her. Or at least a central part of me resisted
hearing her. She might want to categorize this behavior as
not listening, but that sounds more willful than the way I
experienced it. For me it felt like I was being held captive
by an instinctively dissociative response to her words. Certain words, like *remember* and *before* and *again*, or phrases,
like "we've been through this" or "you need to let go,"
were triggering sensations that distracted me from the very
same words that were initiating the response, and this reaction, this disconnection, had a distant familiarity to it,
like hazy memories of feelings falling down to me out of
time from a well-traveled place. I know this doesn't appear
to make much sense. The best way I can describe experiencing this echo from somewhere else in time is if you
imagined a roller coaster that did a full 360-degree loop,
and either it was moving so fast or gravity was so weak
that you could somehow drop something from the top part
of the loop, when you were upside down, and it would
defy the rules of time and fall into your lap at the point in
the past when your car was only just beginning to start the

loop. Or maybe it wasn't the past. Maybe you took the loop so fast that you were actually on your second time around when you caught the thing you had just dropped. You lost count. You were turned around. Down was up. Before was after. Past was future. See, it's confusing, which is probably why I don't bother describing it to people anymore. But just in case, here's another way I have attempted to explain it: As a child you say something to your grandfather and it doesn't make sense to either of you, but you're a child and therefore less rooted in language, which frees you up to say things that are poetic, if also gibberish. And your grandfather kind of laughs at it, because it is meaningful in its amusing, non-sensical way, and the laughter makes you feel good, because it is a form of recognition. And then seventy years later, your grandson says the same thing to you, at least to the best that your tired memory can verify, and it still doesn't make sense, but it does effectively make you wonder which event came first. So, anyway, this happens to me sometimes. Certain words may result in a kind of sizzle in my head, or maybe it's a resizzle. I have come to think of it as a bird with rare markings that keeps showing up at notable moments in my life—funerals, warm nonverbal connections with strangers on a bus, blind dates gone wrong, traffic accidents. The bird is a silent witness to that cousin of the epiphany where you feel a deep awareness of a moment that surrounds you, but minus any improved understanding or clarity regarding why or how we are to be in our lives. Maybe it is pointless to try to explain. It isn't really necessary to the retelling. The gist is: Her mouth was moving. Words were coming out. I felt a familiarity with the experience of falling upward and away from the content of what she was saying, and this transitioned into a fuzzed-out ringing in my eardrums. Alternate words then began to come out of her mouth. These words I *could* hear clearly, though they didn't correspond with the movement of her lips; she was suddenly an actor in a foreign film with the dialogue hastily dubbed in. The new words were saying, "She's trying to tell you things you don't need to hear. People will do this. They will talk you out of what you are trying to do, because they are invested in this illness. But you are onto something. Why else would you be feeling this way? It is the nature of the illness to think you are crazy for suspecting it even exists. That's how it takes over. Fight it. Nod at your wife like you are listening to what she is saying, but in your head know that you will stick with this. You've taken your survey. You saw the answers. This isn't make-believe." It felt good to hear somebody say that, even if nobody was really saying that. It felt good until I looked at her eyes. They were concerned, like I was an injured animal, and even though I suspected she was trying to talk me out of something, I couldn't deny that her eyes were particularly beautiful at this moment. I have overlooked brown. It doesn't have the flash of blue or green, but the browns in her eyes were subtly layered, like the earth, or a delicate sweater knitted by hand—something to support you under your feet and keep you warm at night. Her eyes were trying to reach me, as she pushed an envelope across the table in my direction. And then finally her speech—the speech that was aligned with the movement of her mouth—returned. She said, "I've been holding on to this envelope for you for a while now, and I think the time has come for you to open it." I'm pretty sure that's what she said. That's how I have it ordered in my memory. She passed me an envelope, expressed some concern, and got up with her dishes. That's the pattern. She washes her dishes and leaves for work.

On the way out she swooped in for a kiss to my forehead. As she put on her coat, she looked back at me from the hallway. She paused to say one more thing but instead made a face that was the equivalent of another kiss.

I said, "Have a good day at work," but I could barely hear my voice as I said it.

As she left I stared at her, I stared at her ass in her skirt, and I recalled staring at her ass in college, where we had first met. We were both in the same class: "The History of Science." It fulfilled a requirement. We enjoyed the class. We both appreciated science from a distance. We both liked electricity and birth control. She was the fourth person I had ever slept with, and it was the first time it didn't make me feel like either a baboon or an astronaut. Sleeping with her put me on Earth, and that was a feeling I wanted to marry.

The envelope she had given me had my name on it. It was written in my own handwriting. There was no postage. No return address. I put the envelope in a stack of mail I continue to build on. I have an aversion to bills and other things addressed to me. I avoid opening them until the tower of mail gets so high it begins to spill over. Then I reluctantly face up to it.

I was much more interested in Brenda's survey than the envelope with my name on it. So that's where I shifted my attention:

NAME: BRENDA CHAMPS

Are you single?

Not yet.

Are you having an affair?

Not yet.

Why are you so sad?

Did I say I was sad? I don't think that I did.

When was the last time you felt happy?

When I balanced our checkbook.

Was it a true, pure happy or a relative happy?

It was a you are wasting my fucking time with this survey kind of happy.

Are you who you want to be?

Last I checked.

Would you prefer to be someone else?

I am good at being me. You know that.

Are you similar to the "you" you thought you would become when as a child you imagined your future self?

I thought I might have a house with a swimming pool and a pink Cadillac. I didn't realize my breasts would have a weight to them. I didn't think they would hurt my back. I was a child. I imagined child stuff. This is a dumb question.

Is today worse than yesterday?

All days are the same.

If you were a day of the week, would you be Monday or Wednesday?

Both.

What does it feel like to get out of bed in the morning?

Like popping a joint back into place.

Do you realize you have on average another 11,000 to 18,250 mornings of looking in the mirror and wondering if people will find you attractive?

I think I look great. You better too.
Stop staring in the mirror and do some
push-ups.

**Do you think people will remember you
after you die?**

They better.

For how long after you die?

How would I know?

Do you believe in God?

Kind of. Not really. Sort of.

Do you believe in life after death?

I don't like to think about that.

Do you believe in life after God?

I still believe in God, more or less.
Is that what you are getting at? What
is this about? This is madness.

**Are you for the chemical elimination of
all things painful?**

Look, I took those ones to quit
smoking. And I took those others for my
ankle injury, and I keep around the
extras for the occasional hell-born
menstrual cramp. And those others I

don't take but keep around in case I
need to relax. Like after I see you are
spending your time writing insane
mental-health surveys, which winds me
up, so then I want to take a pill to
wind down. There is nothing wrong with
that.

Do you think we need more sports?

Raymond,

What is this all about? Did you write
up this fake questionnaire because you
thought I didn't hear your paranoid
nonsense the other night? Memo: The
world is still spinning. Everybody is
fine. People are unhappy sometimes.
You'll be fine.

Love,
Brenda

P.S. Don't take this to work. I don't
want to have to support you when you
get fired.

Was she happy? I would say she was not in touch with
her unhappiness. Or maybe she possessed a gene that
helped her resist the decline. She was of a blurred Eastern
European background. There is probably a village some-

where over there where the women all behave like her. They all whistle the same tune while the men and animals fall over dead.

I looked at the clock on the microwave. I was late for work. I find it difficult to move at that hour. Like there are ankle weights on my soul. But I had to move or I would be late, and I was always late.

So I did get up. In a mild act of defiance, I put Brenda's survey in the shredder—the data was corrupted anyway—and spread the confettilike end product in with the kitty litter. It might be more useful there, is what I was thinking. We have a cat. Gus. He's missing a leg. I had wanted to call him Triangles, but Brenda thought that was stupid. It was stupid. That was the point. That cat is stupid.

When was the last time you felt happy?

That's just it. I don't trust my memories anymore. When I think back to times I was happy, was I really happy, or just not quite as sad? I registered them into the mental ledger as happy, but now if I could graph it, my fondest memories might actually chart in a negative quadrant. An example: My father allegedly spent his nights taking care of his mother. He was a lawyer and he worked all day. Sometimes he came home for lunch or to drop off his dirty laundry, but most of the week he was at work or with his mother. Nobody was more insistent about this being true than my mother. I once said, "Can he really be spending all of his nights with Grandma?" and my mother looked at me with an insane fierceness. She said, "Your grandmother is very sick. Your father is a saint for treating her so well. I hope that I am never that sick, but if I am, I hope you take care of me as well as your father takes care of your grandmother." Except my father had a nurse to take care of his mother. And additionally, we had a spare

room in our house my grandmother could
have stayed in, but for some reason
didn't. In any event, he always came
home for a big Sunday meal. My mother
would cook a whole hen, or a roast, or
something she could bring out on a plat-
ter and make a fuss over. It was always
a big occasion. And my father would sit
at the table and ask me about my grades,
and when I was done telling him how hard
I had worked, he would give me a pack of
baseball cards, even though what I really wanted were art supplies. But it
didn't matter, because I was willing to
try to like baseball. I memorized statistics and would talk to him about the
statistics, and he seemed on those afternoons to be proud of me. I remember
thinking at the time, This is happy.

D on Ables was in my cubicle fishing through the
basket of surveys. His back was to me. Under a
striped corporate-casual shirt, he had the shoulders of a sea mammal. Rounded and hydrodynamic.

He said, still facing the other direction, "I don't agree
with what I wrote yesterday."

"Did you wake up knowing more about yourself?"

"No."

I was disappointed.

I could see that he had located his survey. He held it up
and looked it over and shook his head in disapproval.

"I'll bring this right back," he said, and left.

The light on my phone was flashing. It was a voice
mail from Brenda: *It's me . . . Why aren't you at work yet? Did
you stop off and watch a movie or something? . . . How are you
able to keep a job? . . . Did you open the envelope? . . . I was wondering how you are feeling . . . and . . . you know . . . how it felt
to read the letter . . . Call me if you need to . . . Love you . . . Bye.*

I thought about what she said long enough to forget what she said, and then started working on a drawing for a bedside table that doubled as a doghouse. I wasn't doing well. The dog looked like he was losing his vision. His eyes looked glazed and dumb. The nightstand/doghouse was flimsy. It was like a shanty out on the far edges of an over-grown capital; there was no infrastructure for this poor dog, or for all of the farmworkers who had moved to the big city on a false rumor. Just a cheap house that I couldn't draw very well.

I looked up at the photo of the African boy with the gun and said, "Can you imagine having a credit card in your child soldier name and buying a house for your dog made out of particleboard on borrowed money that you would have to pay back at a twenty-two percent annual percentage rate?"

He said, *Hell no.*

Then he just looked like he wanted to shoot me.

Sometimes I can't sit still. Particularly when the little soldier is staring at me. At those times I go get coffee or potato chips, or I wash my hands, or I contemplate taking up smoking, or I walk outside to the parking lot and sit in my car and listen to music, or lately just listen to the parking lot, since my stereo was stolen.

I passed Don's cube on my way to the parking lot. There were photos of Alan Alda pinned to the walls. He looked to be hard at work on the survey. When he became aware that I could see him, he shielded the survey even though there was no chance I could read it from the edge of

his cube. I leaned in across the threshold without technically entering and said, "Don, if you want to talk about the
survey, I am here for you."

For a moment I got caught in the gaze of his sister in
that terrible photo. It looked like she was trying to wink
but didn't know how. Because Don was still silent, I said,
"Do you think there are people who are unable to wink?"

He kept on writing. I could see he was crossing out
large sections of the survey.

He said, "Are there any more blank copies of this?"

I said, "I don't know. I'd have to ask Jerry."

He had a large black marker in one hand and a ballpoint pen in the other. Blacking out and writing new answers and blacking out. I didn't know whether to stay or
leave. I thought it was sad that we never really had conver-
sations about anything real or true. The only things we
talked about were the latest e-mails about sick leave policy
and whether we had a favorite freeway.

I said, "Any word on what they are serving for lunch
today?"

"Don't know." He wrote some more; I hovered waiting
for something. I thought about inviting him out to my car,
but then decided against it.

"Ray, who reads these surveys?"

"I think it is a project that Bob Grasston is heading up."

"Then why are you collecting them?"

"Doctor's orders," I said, and shrugged like it was all
part of a needlessly bureaucratic protocol that would be a
waste of time to try to understand.

"But you aren't going to read them, are you?"

"Me?"

"Yeah. Who reads them?"

"I don't know. I could barely read mine, it was so boring. Maybe this is something they have to do for insurance purposes. Maybe it's a way of covering their tracks or something. You know, physical evidence that they at least once asked how we're doing. I don't really know. They probably picked me because I'm at the end of the aisle."

Despite an obvious dissatisfaction with my explanation, he handed me his survey.

"I'll add it to the others," I said, and gave him a salute as if we were both in the military. I hated myself for making the gesture.

His survey was a mess. The original answers were blacked out. I ducked into the men's bathroom and attempted to decipher the answers in one of the stalls. It was quiet and clean in there. Almost unused. Nothing was written on the putty-gray walls that divided the toilets. I had to tilt the paper at just the right angle so that the light would reflect the grooves of the original ballpoint answers, which were now covered in wide swaths of ink. It was difficult to make out all of it, and Don's penmanship wasn't great to begin with.

NAME: DON ABLES

Are you single?

I live with my sister, Geraldine.

Are you having an affair?

I am not married.

This is where his revisions began, the original, crossed-out answers followed by the new ones.

Are you who you want to be?

~~I always wanted to be a surgeon in the Korean War.~~
Yes.

Would you prefer to be someone else?

~~I wish I had a nickname like Eagle Eyes or Sonar.~~
I am perfectly fine being me.

Are you similar to the "you" you thought you would become when as a child you imagined your future self?

~~I thought I would end up in a prison. I always thought I would wake up and my parents would be dead. And then I would owe the money on the house and car and would be sent to prison because I couldn't pay off their debts with my newspaper-delivery earnings, and I feared that in prison they would ▮▮▮ me or I would ▮▮ until I couldn't ▮▮▮ anymore.~~
I imagined keeping a job and having an apartment, so yes.

Why are you so sad?

~~I don't hang out with a group of pals. I~~
~~long for camaraderie. Somebody to play~~
~~practical jokes on.~~
I am not sad.

When was the last time you felt happy?

~~When my~~ ████ ~~was~~ ██ ~~and I loved~~ █████
~~so much, it felt so good it hurt me in my~~
██ ~~, but in the nicest way. But that was~~
~~such a long time ago.~~
Driving to work this morning.

**Was it a true, pure happy or a relative
happy?**

~~Are temporary things pure?~~
It seemed fine.

**If you were a day of the week, would you
be Monday or Wednesday?**

~~"M.A.S.H." is on both nights.~~
Both.

Somebody entered the bathroom. I feared, though I
knew it to be highly unlikely, that somehow the other occupant would know that I was sitting on the toilet with my
pants on. Nobody had ever peeked in on me in all my years
of sitting in bathroom stalls, but I noted a minor rise in internal panic. The occupant hovered quietly over a urinal

and then washed his hands. He lingered in front of the mirror. I could see through the crack, between the stall door and the wall, that the stranger was wearing a pink oxford shirt and had brown hair. I waited quietly. I made no noises. Is that what I would do if I were really using the toilet? Should I be making fake noises? I wasn't sure. At last, he left.

I returned to my deciphering.

Do you realize you have on average another 11,000 to 18,250 mornings of looking in the mirror and wondering if people will find you attractive?

~~I look in the mirror and think about another forty years of people simply finding me in their field of vision and then making excuses about something they have to do.~~
I don't spend a lot of time in front of the mirror.

Do you think people will remember you after you die?

~~No.~~
Yes.

For how long after you die?

██████████~~.~~
As long as those people who remember me live.

Do you believe in God?

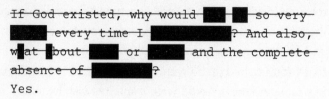

~~If God existed, why would ▓▓ ▓ so very~~
~~▓▓▓ every time I ▓▓▓▓▓▓▓▓? And also,~~
~~w▓at ▓bout ▓▓▓ or ▓▓▓▓ and the complete~~
~~absence of ▓▓▓▓▓?~~
Yes.

Do you believe in life after God?

I don't understand the question.

Here he stuck with his original answer. Perhaps I should rephrase that question.

Are you for the chemical elimination of all things painful?

~~I am afraid of taking drugs. Alcohol makes~~
~~me feel out of control. That is the only~~
~~drug I have tried except for allergy~~
~~medicine.~~
No.

Do you think we need more sports?

~~Sports have only ▓▓▓▓ and ▓▓▓▓.~~
If it is good for the country or the company, why not?

I was both encouraged by Don's initial openness to the survey and discouraged by his revisions. It corrupted my results. I had naively anticipated a certain level of honesty.

I wondered what Don would do if I started calling him Sonar. I wondered if I shouldn't use the toilet since I had already been there. I dropped my pants, and did the things
we do—unnecessary to elaborate on, I'm sure. Let's say
that I found a peace. I played a game I like to play with my
memory, where I insert fantasized memories back into my
life, altering its course, but feeling deeply that it's almost
real, or certainly would have transpired that way, had I just
made a few different moves. I rolled back in time. Instead
of a life with Brenda—with whom I still allowed myself a
short-lived, sex-filled fling in my revised past, just not one
that involved marriage—I asked Hope Crestwell out on a
date, which, because I did so in such a charming way, led
to much, much more. Hope had been the most talented artist in the life-drawing class I audited at the art academy.
She had this way of confidently not caring about anything.
Like the teacher would tell her to change something, to
make it more proportionally faithful, but she knew she
didn't need to listen to the teacher, and she continued to
draw the models both as they were and also in ways they
were not. So a thin woman in her thirties with small, pear-
shaped breasts would in Hope's drawing look larger than
a bear, maybe even with fur, but still exactly like herself.
And the idiotic teacher would tell her not to do that. The
point is that this made Hope irresistible. She knew who she
was, or maybe didn't give a shit about who she wasn't.
And I pictured us living in France with our very quiet,
well-mannered child, who liked to entertain herself in the
outdoors collecting butterflies while Hope and I made love

in a rustic but charming farmhouse filled with exotic canvases where we were each making really bold, fearless brushstrokes. Then my daydream came to an end when I noticed there was only a cube and a half of toilet paper left on the roll.

Are you similar to the "you" you thought you would become when as a child you imagined your future self?

No. My favorite fantasy was that I was going to invent trains that would let me see the world, and that something to do with this invention would allow me to be a wealthy, train-riding philanthropist. I hadn't worked out the economic feasibility of this daydream. I was only ten. I knew the train would be silver and purple and that it would have different recreational cars—a jungle gym car, a swimming pool car, a trampoline car, a milk shake car. To get between the cars you would have to crawl through orange plastic tubes. One of the cars, the aviary car, would be made entirely of glass and be full of talking birds that could tell jokes even if they didn't know what the jokes meant. The train would be able to go anywhere, but mostly it would go through wild monkey reserves and futuristic cities. I would invite beautiful women along and there would be something romantic or affectionate in these invitations and their company, but at ten I didn't understand exactly how this ro-

mance would function. Mostly it involved
the beautiful women being impressed with
me and the monkey reserves, and possess-
ing an enthusiastic willingness to play
any game that I wanted to play.

At my desk, more thoughts of Don soared on the shifting air currents in my head. The life he probably lived. Nights in front of the television. Geraldine, a quiet presence. Her eyebrow arched with concern for wartime medicine. I imagined they kept their rooms dark. That they read magazines to the light of the TV. That they wore custom slippers. I entertained these thoughts while I worked on a drawing for a combination CD rack/shoe organizer. In my drawing the rack was beginning to look like an accordion, an instrument I've always admired. I gave it a face. The face had big cheeks, ready to puff out stale air. I put the drawing aside, looked at my phone—no messages—glanced at the photos on the wall—still there. I blew my nose. Cleared my throat. Cracked my knuckles. Played a game of online poker. An e-mail came, asking people to give blood. Another arrived, alerting us to a health insurance deadline that involved a date and a form. A third warned that they were spraying pesticides along the campus pathways over the weekend, which should not constitute a health hazard except for any employees who might be pregnant.

I left my desk to hide out in my car for a while. I sat there wishing I still had a stereo, thinking I ought to buy a new one, then talking to myself, putting my head in my hands, putting my hands behind my head, adjusting the seat backward, and then forward a bit, and then too far forward, and then back a little. A small motor buzzed in the direction of my car. A man in a jumpsuit and hard ear-muffs was wrangling leaves with a leaf blower. It was still summer. I don't know why he thought there would be a lot of leaves. His machine was loud. It hung from a strap that went over his shoulder. The exhaust from the blower danced upward in translucent heat. I watched him weaving through the sea of cars, back and forth, like he was a shark circling for chum. Then he came out of the water and started to blow nearer the building. As I tracked his move-ments I noticed Robin Lipsk sitting at the picnic table next to the wheelchair ramp. She had been watching me. Robin was the one female member of tech support. They were a cartel. They kept their own schedules, and they all agreed to act with a casual concern toward everything. They had all the power.

Robin was an enigma. A convergence of science fiction enthusiasm, confrontational tattoos, and computer fluency. She wore strange beads around her neck. Maybe they were teeth and not beads. It looked like she had paid disabled children to cut her hair. She had dyed it pink and green, probably without realizing those were also the company colors.

She walked up to my car. Stared through the window. I smiled and raised my eyebrows to acknowledge her, hoping she would walk away. She opened the door and got in.

"Let me smoke in your car."

I didn't respond. I tried to look uncomfortable, which didn't take much effort.

She said, "I'll bump you up on the waiting list for the new machines."

"Smoke away."

"It's kind of dirty in here," she said, pulling a glass pipe out of her army surplus pants, followed by a sizable green bud that was silhouetted in miniature orange hairs. It was the professional athlete of the plant world. It looked like it had been meeting with a trainer who fed it a cocktail of illicit enhancements in preparation for the competition that was about to take place in Robin's head. She groomed the bud like a Zen butcher who could carve a shank with her eyes closed, never hitting the bone. And then the car filled with smoke. She offered me some. I declined. She started looking through my glove compartment.

"Can I help you find something?"

"Don't you have anything to listen to?"

"Just the leaf blower."

She smoked some more. We watched the leaf blower through the rearview mirror. The man didn't smile. He was smoking a cigarette while he worked. He wasn't even looking at where he was blowing, as far as I could tell.

"He has a rad mustache," she said.

"It will not blow away," I said.

She looked at me like I had said something special, something heavy, instead of realizing I was just trying to get through this.

"I like your car."

"Thanks."

"My mom has one like this."

"Is your mom happy?"

"I don't know."

We sat. She started to complain about the leader of the tech support cartel, Kyle Blanks. He was a real selfish dick. I asked if he was happy. She didn't think he was, or more accurately, she hoped he wasn't. Then she was transfixed by a passing cloud that she thought looked like a bagpipe. She thought bagpipes were freaky but also beautiful.

"It sounds like they are crying, 'cause they can never get rid of that one note. It drones on, like a broken key."

I started to like her. This was better than e-mail.

She made the flame of her lighter curve toward the bowl as she sucked in more drug. It made a crinkling sound: baby sticks on fire. As the smoke came out she said, "Do you think time has a shape? I mean, duh, of course it does, but what shape do you think it has?"

"Maybe like Kansas? I don't know. I never thought about it."

"Never? Kansas? You mean like a real flat plane?" I didn't answer, so she went on. "I think it is shaped like a bow tie, but I think most people think it is shaped like a rake."

"Well, then I think it is shaped like a frown."

I could feel smoke entering my tear ducts.

"You mean like it is linear but it swells upward in the present and then back down again in the future?"

"Maybe more like the downward motion of an airplane that has run out of fuel."

She said, "Most people think everything up until now is a line. And some think the future is also a straight line. But some think right after this moment the future fans out in various directions. The tines of the rake are the different paths available to us in the future." Her eyes were spinning like fruits in a slot machine.

"Do they continue to exist in multiples after they are absorbed by the present?"

"Good question," she said, giving me a friendly punch in the shoulder to punctuate her appreciation. We were friends now. Maybe. Don would be jealous because he had once tried to talk to Robin about *Lost in Space* and she hadn't been interested. And because now my computer would get fixed faster than his.

We looked out at the clouds again. I pointed to one that I thought looked like a shoe. She saw it as a croissant.

"But if the future fans out, wouldn't the past also fan out?" she said. "That's what I think. Think about it. It's like trees: If you dig in the ground, they don't go down in a straight line; the roots below stretch out like the branches above. Right? We are totally perched on the nose of a cat, and the future and the past are the whiskers."

"My cat only has three legs."

"Aw."

"If you are right about the tines, does that mean that it would be possible for all of us to die off in one tine but live on in another? Is there a tine where we all live underwater and coexist with aquatic tigers?"

She wasn't listening. She was staring at a couple walking back to the building from the far end of the parking lot. The man was adjusting his shirt. The woman was fixing her hair. It was Nora and Charlie. They walked past us, too involved with each other to notice us staring at them through caged smoke. I looked over at Robin. She was gazing at Nora. Her mouth was open the way my mouth is open when I realize I have been staring at Nora and then look around to make sure nobody has seen me. Robin had the same open mouth.

It erased our conversation. Wiped it out. She said she had to go back inside to install a sort of software something. I went back to rework the drawing that wasn't supposed to be of an accordion. We didn't talk. We walked past the leaf shepherd, who was now sitting at the picnic table eating a banana. We entered the building and fanned off in our separate directions.

There appeared to be a few more surveys in the envelope, but not enough. I wanted more. I wanted to leave. I left.

Are you for the chemical elimination of all things painful?

It sounds good on paper, but dulling the painful would dull the soft, would dull the pretty, would dull the surprising, would dull the songs, would dull the laughter, and all this dulling would end in a sum that registered on the color scale as a beige that caused birth defects in lab mice. But yes, I like pills.

I was in the video store, wading in an overflow of consumer stimuli. Flattened screens were making claims about high definitions. Animated insects were talking like stand-up comedians while falling into sharpened computer foliage. Cardboard cutouts promoted the competing romantic comedies of the decade.

A woman with her dog was on the phone asking what she should bring home, reading the backs of boxes aloud into the phone. "This one's got Pierce Brosnan," she said, "*and* a love triangle." Her dog wasn't happy. He probably smelled rat poison or was irritated by the high-pitched noise that was broadcast every time a customer came in or out of the store. I hoped in vain that the dog would shit on the carpet, which was patterned in dancing film reels. I hated the carpet. I hated the woman. And I recognized that was mean-spirited. I wondered if I should put that on the next revision of the emotional self-appraisal.

—*Have you always been mean-spirited?*

—*Would you attribute your mean spirit to nature or nurture?*

—*Have you ever wanted someone or something to fail for reasons that were not entirely clear to you? Perhaps a restaurant that played techno music while you attempted to digest your food, or a man who wore open-toed shoes into that same restaurant?*

Holding a copy of a direct-to-video movie about a traffic accident that brought together strangers who were both recently widowed, I contemplated a few more:

—*Is all communication impossible?*

—*Do you wonder if words like* face, blue, happy, exceptional, honest, magical, heart, wish, love, *and* please *may mean something else to other people, but because everybody is consistent in what they think the terms mean, it is very difficult to detect that we are in fact referring to different concepts and feelings?*

—*For instance, you meet someone, and you say you like to travel and they say that they like to travel, do you nevertheless feel like the ways in which they like to travel are not the same as the ways in which you like to travel?*

—*And more importantly, why does that make you feel so completely alone in the world?*

I browsed in a different direction from the woman and her poor mutt. We were like ducks on a pond, watercraft drifting along fifty-some years of Hollywood spew. At the end of the aisle were buckets of popcorn, boxes of candy, and some tabloid magazines. Despite zero interest in its contents, I found myself picking up *Them Weekly*. A new reality person was rumored to be drinking while pregnant. I put the magazine back and thought of a few more questions:

> —*To relieve yourself from boredom, do you distract*
> *yourself with things that are also boring?*
> —*Are you more afraid of boredom or death?*
> —*If you could represent your most horrifying boredom*
> *with a sound, what would it be? A drip? A scream?*
> *The cryptic chirp of an outdated modem?*

My drift had taken me toward the front of the store. A clerk in a blue shirt with the yellow Movie Blitz logo was behind the counter giving a minimum-wage effort. She was dipping fast food into fast sauces, leafing through a magazine, not paying attention to anything outside of the glossy photos, dipping nuggets into sauces without even looking, but never missing. She did this with great long painted fingernails that seemed like a place I would call home if I were a flesh-eating bacteria. She always dipped first into a semitranslucent amber sauce—three quick dips and then a longer, lingering plunge into a darker and thicker sauce that I presumed was barbecue. I was transfixed, watching her hands carry the food to her mouth; entirely captivated, like a child at the zoo, watching closely to see how an animal could possibly entertain itself in such cramped quarters; wondering if the animal knew it wasn't in its natural habitat. And I was incredibly curious to see how long she could eat this way without missing, or if she would ever break from her pattern with the dips and the sauces. I couldn't decide which side of the event I was rooting for. Was I hoping for the pitcher to throw a perfect game, or was I waiting to see if the race car drivers would crash in flames? Would she dip a nugget into the cash drawer, or smear sauce on the magazine, or miss her mouth altogether and smear it on her face? And what could possibly be in the magazine? Nothing was in the magazine. But she was looking at it like they were having a conversation.

She finally caught wind of me watching her like an animal, so I asked her what she recommended.

"I don't know. What do you like?" she said, and dipped.

"I need to make my wife trust me again."

"We have some video games where you can shoot people together."

"I was thinking more of a movie."

"New movies are over there. Most people like the new releases." She was looking at the magazine as she said it. I wanted to go into the back room with her and eat some of those terribly sour sugar worms together, to get a younger and poorer perspective on just how bad things were.

"And I just so happen to be looking for a new release on life."

It is amazing how before you say something, you think it is a sensible thing to say, but even as your lips are turning the thought into sound, you begin to realize what a terrible thing you're about to say. It was a poor joke. Not even a joke—a pun. Younger people hate puns, especially coming from older people.

My cell phone rang. I nodded at the clerk, as if regrettably this damned device was bringing our conversation to a premature end, and moved over to a shelf organized by the theme of violence with cars.

"Did you find something yet?"

"I just got here."

I could sense Brenda was walking around on the other end of the call. I don't know how. It's part of the dark science behind marriage. I couldn't hear her opening our refrigerator, but I knew that's what she was doing, and that she was pouring herself some filtered water, and when she was done with that, she would stare into the fridge looking for something to eat, like if she waited long enough there might be some activity in there, but then after staring for some time, she would shut the door without taking anything out.

"Why didn't you open the envelope I gave you this morning?"

"What envelope?"

"Raymond!" She sounded exasperated. I told her that Triangles, I mean Gus, distracted me and then I was late for work. Was that true? It seemed like it was essentially true. Then neither of us said anything. Now I couldn't hear but knew she was sitting at the kitchen table looking through the mail.

"After everything I said this morning?"

"You know how Gus gets." This was as pathetic as the pun I made for the nugget-eater.

I could detect, with my marital sense, that she was taking off her shoes and rubbing her feet, and I had always suspected that when she did this, she would press extra hard on the really tender points and imagine her feet were like voodoo dolls, and that by pinching them in such a focused way, she was inflicting a corresponding pain in my shoulders or my testicles or any part of my anatomy that deserved justice.

"Well, just rent some fucking movie and come home."

"I will."

"Make it funny, but not jokey."

"I'll try."

"But hurry up. I'm getting tired."

"Why don't I just come home and we can talk?" I surprised myself.

"I am afraid of what you will say."

"What will I say?"

"That your life is over, or that you wish you had become a magician, or that you think we should become nudists, or something else that is divorced from reality."

"I won't say anything." I made a mental note to add a question about divorce and reality in the next revision of the survey.

—Are you divorced from reality?
—What made you get married in the first place?
—Were you pressured into it?

I was about to start reading her titles from the new release section, but then I realized I would become the
woman with the dog.

"What's taking you so long?"

"Well, at first it was that the clerk had a fascinating eating ritual, and it captivated me. I think you would understand if you saw her." I whispered this very carefully. "And
then it made me think of the zoo."

"See, that's the kind of thing you will say."

But it was true. I thought about the day my dad took
me to the zoo and how the wolverine had lain next to a
leafless tree, as if it was wounded—and perhaps it had
been. It was the only visible wolverine—this wasn't a big-
budget zoo—and it looked like it had fallen from the sky
right onto a small patch of cost-effective ground cover. And
I was a kid. I didn't understand why a wolverine would be
splayed out and inert. I wanted an explanation. I said,
"Dad?" And he said, "I know, I know, this is a disgrace. We
paid ten bucks and all the animals play dead." He said that
after seeing the wolverine, but it was even worse when we
came to the elephant. The elephant was in a mental rut. He
was moving, but his brain had crashed. This was probably
my first exposure to insanity, or at least the palpable strain
that is right out in front of you. He was big and gray and
majestic, as all elephants are, but despair radiated off his

giant body. He took a step backward and then he took a
step forward. He only looked in front of him, toward the
fence that separated him from the giraffes. His trunk hung
low. He took another step backward. He took a step forward. He repeated this motion while the zookeeper, help-
less, tried to sell him on the hope of walking in a full circle
around the faux rock enclave. *Come on, elephant, you can do
it!* But the elephant was completely broken. I had no idea
how they would fix him. It was terrifying. He was broken
like my radio-controlled car, which had gotten too much
hair and dirt caught in its wheelbase and as a result could
never turn right or go in reverse. The elephant's gears were
broken: Forward half a step. Backward half a step. Pause.
Look bewildered by own brokenness. Repeat until death. I
wanted to cry, but I thought that might make it worse; that
my tears might confirm that the elephant couldn't be fixed.
My dad took me away and said, "This is worse than taxi-
dermy."

The epidemic was beginning all the way back then. I
had been too young to piece it all together. I was nine and
I knew the animals were telling me something, but I
couldn't figure out exactly what. I didn't realize then that it
wasn't just confined to the zoo.

"Are you still there?"

"Yes, I'm looking at the cover of a movie with Woody
Harrelson. He plays a blind man." I was as bad as the
woman with the dog. I looked for her and the dog—well,
really just for the dog—wanting to get a look at its face, see
if it was carrying a mournful countenance or trembling in

fear of a gutted future that hadn't yet registered with our dim senses, but the dog was gone.

"Is it jokey?"

"I can't tell. Hold on. It says 'heartfelt.'"

"Ew."

"They have two whole shelves of *Titanic Returns*."

"How could they make a sequel of that? Didn't everybody die?"

"Maybe it's about reincarnation."

"Oh, it doesn't matter. Just come home."

I decided I would get a couple of movies so that she could choose. I rented *The Wind* with Lillian Gish. A silent film from 1928. The box said it was about a woman who moves to west Texas, where she is plagued by a howling wind and marriage proposals. I also rented *Kramer vs. Kramer*. I didn't read the cover on that one, but I remembered liking it some time ago, and I knew that Brenda liked legal thrillers.

The clerk scanned the movies with a bar code gun that was tethered to her computer. She did it without looking at me. She was chewing gum. Had she been chewing gum while eating the nuggets? It seemed possible. I said, since I had no credibility left to lose after the pun, "Do you think that historians lie about the past to make the present look better than it is?"

She said, "That'll be seven dollars and ninety-eight cents."

Do you believe in life after God?

I am trying to. I still like to eat food.
You don't need God to enjoy an avocado.

A warm loaf of bread is on my chest. A thermal whole-grain weight that vibrates. Is this bad or good? I should care for the bread. If I move the bread is spoiled. Falls onto the floor of cabin. Cabin that is black and white, with doors banging from howling wind. Beautiful, pale woman runs back and forth distressed. A terrified doll in a ruffled dress. She doesn't see me. Why can't she see the lovely loaf of bread I protect like a baby?

I was on the sofa, drifting and dreaming. Brenda had left me sleeping there to the accompaniment of a rental decision that lacked a joint enthusiasm. Lillian Gish was flickering like a star, getting blown about in a rustic shack. Gus was on my chest, his quiet motor spinning inside, pinning me down. Asleep. What time was it? Was I still depressed? Was Gus? I think he was not yet infected, bless his three-legged heart. I kicked off my shoes. I eyed a blanket on the arm of the chair next to the couch. With the caution of a tightrope walker, I reached for the blanket, hoping not to disrupt my sleeping loaf. We drifted out again.

I give Lillian the questionnaire. Her face glows white like an exquisite mushroom that blossoms in a dark forest far away from the sun. Her body, because the lord was once merciful, has never seen a gym. I can admire its outline through her historical nightgown. I hand her a piece of paper. It has only one question on it: *Did people have more or less free time prior to the invention of abs?*

Gus moved to a space that was both my shoulder and the side of my face. Awoken, I watched the end of the picture. I fell in love with Lillian and wondered if it was possible for people to look like that today. If Brenda and I abandoned our promise to each other and decided to have a child, and that child blossomed into a beautiful star of the silent screen, would she be destroyed by a tanning booth? I watched the finale of the picture. I could tell I would sleep again soon. Reading the interstitial titles to the plink of an old-timey piano was a much more effective relaxant than staring at the ceiling fan next to a wife who sleeps like a determined snowbank.

Are you who you want to be?

No. I want to exist in a moment. In this moment I will not feel unease. I will not long for anything but that exact emotional location in space and time. I will be content with what I am, with where and when and who I am, and I will care very little about past and future. I will not cling to my anxieties. I will not act like a child. I will not act like my father when Brenda reminds me of my mother. If I hold Brenda, my hands will feel it. And Brenda too will feel it, and enjoy feeling it. And no matter what she says, I will feel without defense or anger or guilt, or if I feel those things I will be confident that those feelings are true, and by knowing they are true those feelings will no longer trap me or shame me. Every action, whether positive or negative, will be like a note in a complex chord that we will both love and understand. We will revere this miraculous chord that holds everything inside of it; we will grow symbiotically, toward the light of the chord, toward the light of the realization that to feel is to understand, and vice versa. We will breathe together. And all of it will be lovely; even the saddest parts will be lovely, especially the saddest parts, because I will be there for every note. And hopefully so will Brenda. She'll be newly captivated by this more essential me. And this load we carry—the anger, the fatigue, the resentment, and the deathly sense of compromise that is bound to our backs or held tightly in our clenched fists—it will still exist, but we won't have to carry it, because it belongs to the past or the future, and that's not where we'll be. We will experience more, and it will weigh less. Nothing will be under a microscope or in a photograph or forgotten in some dusty file. Everything will be in us, vibrating harmonically in our bones. But I have no idea how any of this will happen, which makes me think maybe I wouldn't mind being famous and getting into really nice restaurants and flying around on empty jets.

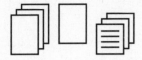

I took the Henry Ford Memorial Bridge that morning. A container ship from China was working its way up the bay, a floating mosaic of painted boxes in weathered reds and faded blues, all filled with lead dog food and tainted pacifiers. Tufts of smoke trailed behind the ship, rising up above the bridge's suspension cables, tucking themselves into the haze. I watched the road curve downward to the other side of the bay and thought about my head—how it felt like it could fall off and nobody would care. Probably because they barely cared that their own heads were about to fall off. The airport was ahead of me. The grass along the runway looked tired of being green. An airplane up in the sky to my left was small but became huge in seconds, cracking the sky in sound, touching down onto the runway that ran alongside the freeway. It was big enough to eat me.

A truck was overturned and on fire just south of the airport. Traffic slowed. Magenta flares dotted the road. It smelled of burning plastic. People were hungry to see the damage. I too would look. I wanted to know what fate I had escaped.

The driver was talking to a police officer, waving his hands about. His shirt was torn and he looked like he had been shaken upside down by a giant. He didn't know if the conversation with the officer was taking place before or after his death. I felt sorry for him, but not as if he was something that actually existed. He was on the other side of the windshield.

Allied Heat and Invisibles, our corporate neighbor, appeared to be having a sales rally. A banner reading, "Innovations in Solution Creations!" was draped along the entrance to the giant prisms of glass and steel that contained their offices. I passed their buildings and pulled in the drive to our campus. There was no place to park. The out-of-town sales reps from Allied had taken over our lot. I thought I saw a spot next to one of the huge machines that pump the airless breezes into our buildings, but it was taken up by a motorcycle that hadn't been visible at first. I circled and circled.

My only option was the Di$count Xplosions parking lot on the other side of the expressway. They always had spaces. I parked in an empty row next to a pen of shopping carts.

Crossing the first half of the expressway, on foot, back toward our offices, was not a problem. The southbound traffic was light. A dirty heat rose off the pavement. I made my way across to the median, but there I was forced to

pause. The northbound traffic was a different beast altogether. It had a homicidal intensity to it. Trucks and cargo
vans looked like they would fly off their axles and take out
my limbs. It was loud. My hair blew. I sneezed, an involun-
tary response to light shining off things. A near guarantee
to make me sneeze, the glimmer of airborne particles. I
searched my pockets for a tissue. Neither pant pocket was
stocked. I tried the breast pocket on my shirt, also finding
no tissues, but the search did inadvertently set free a small
photo I had cut out and placed there for safekeeping. It was
a photo of a mutant frog, a grayish-white cyclops born near
a bio-enhanced fertilizer plant. I wanted it for my cubicle
wall. But it blew free of my hands, fluttering in the shimmering dust. I chased it down, almost getting my hand on
it as it danced in the automotive winds, but then I sneezed
again, the light bouncing against something aluminum. In
only a millisecond I lost the trail of my renegade photo. It
was a terrible place to lose something so scrappy and trash-
like. I got down low, on my hands and knees, figuring it
couldn't have floated far, and searched in the very unique
traffic median ecosystem, where half-items regularly ex-
pire without memorial. A broken toy. Bits of polystyrene.
Rugged plant life. Dirt. Shredded nothings. Eroded some-
things. An orange plastic cap, cracked and punctured.
Filthy strings. An abandoned fast-food prize—a plastic
chicken nugget, perhaps—with eyes and pretend lipstick.
Nowhere could I find the photo. Which was sad. The frog
was sad, which is why I had saved it; it was sad, but igno-
rant about its sadness. Another resolute message to all of

us. We wanted to pretend we weren't like the frog. You know, we have two eyes, we think, our skin has at least some pigment—so we're still doing okay. But like the frog we were born into strange shapes that we merely accept as sensible. Flaps for feet. Ears that are sealed off. Bifurcated tongues. We feel sorry for the frog, but how do we know we aren't ourselves mutations? Anyway, I was looking forward to seeing how it might fit in with the other friends on my wall. I searched just a little bit longer. Brushing away some litter—a potato chip bag, a crumpled beer can, a losing lottery ticket—I noticed a tiny flower in the weeds. It was also a weed, but it was transcendent. The petals were the color of egg yolks but with metallic red edges. It seemed to have no sense of its surroundings, fertilized by snack wrappers and soft drink coupons, respiring an air that hosted a growing number of inorganic particles, drinking up a sun that was forever in polluted veils. The plant persisted despite the odds, and I was inspired. It was not that flowers were new to me. But this flower at this juncture struck a chord. Plants don't always have it easy. They get stepped on and driven over and their terrain is forever encroached upon by asphalt and concrete, but they persevere, and they make these eloquent, fragile sexual organs that we cut and bundle and give to our sweethearts. In that moment, I was willing to get old for the flowers; not for my job, or my wife, or the promise I made to the therapist I fired, but for these little miracles. I could move to the country and have a garden and tickle my nose with daffodils. Maybe Brenda wouldn't come along. Maybe I would leave her behind. She was like an electric blanket I had bought in Europe and now couldn't plug into North American outlets.

I stood up and waited for a break in the traffic. A teenager without sleeves leaned out of a pickup and yelled, "Get a car!" I was too slow to give him the finger. I said, "Fuck you," but I couldn't hear it over the traffic. A space opened in the fluid masses, and I made it across to the offices with all my limbs intact.

Is today worse than yesterday?

Yes, because one of the two I still have
to live through.

AN E-MAIL from my boss was waiting for me:

Ray,

We need to talk. ASAP.

—Jerry

P.S. Be my buddy and bring me a coffee when you come to my office. Black. Two packets of sugar. Thanks, soldier.

My hunch was that Jerry's e-mail had to do with the survey. Maybe it had spoken to him. Unearthed some truths. Jerry was sad. He had to be. Looking at him made me sad. His big head. The brown suits. His misguided sense of self-worth. Sometimes it made me enjoy looking at him, because I felt less sad about myself. But of course that was a trap, no doubt an aspect of the global virus that kept people complacent. *Things can't be so bad, because I am definitely not as bad off as that guy.* It didn't matter who that guy was.

I would go into Jerry's office and he would be crying and I would hold him and say, "We lost a lot of years in this place." He would wipe his tears on his pink and green tie and nod in agreement, and then I would say, "Now what do you say we go out there into the world and start picking up the litter?" We would give each other a rousing high five and kick over his computer in defiant victory. Then he would say, "On second thought, I better stay here and run the shop while you go on the paid leave of absence I will be giving you, because you deserve it. You go out there and figure this nasty swamp bug out. Make some calls. Do some studies. Alert the scientific community. Meanwhile, I'll make sure things are running here so we can afford to subsidize your important work."

Brenda called in the middle of my daydream.

"What are you doing?"

"Talking to you."

"I hate it when you say that. Then I have to say, 'What else?' and then you finally answer the question. You act like I am wasting your time by asking you what you are doing, but your game wastes more time."

"I'm sorry, let's try again."

"What are you doing?"

"Wasting time."

She hung up.

The break room had once been the floor model of a two- to four-person Winnebago. They appended it to the west side of the building, putting a tent between the two so that you

were never technically outside. The Winnebago had been a
luxury item they never expected would sell well, but they
had anticipated, and correctly so, that people would want
to look inside, and would then find themselves purchasing
brand-new picnic baskets and collapsible furniture. When
they finally discontinued the Winnebagos, a manager in a
meeting decided that using one would spice up our workspace while saving on the expense of renovating the old
break room. He was promoted the next day.

There was barely a kitchen in the room. There was a
microwave, and a toaster oven, and a vending machine
where the toilet once had been. There were packets of instant coffees and powdered sweeteners arranged in tidy
rows. There was a half-size refrigerator that was dangerous to open, because it was filled with forgotten yogurts.
And there was Nora, standing alone by the sink, humming
quietly to herself in a minor key.

Her back was to me. She was facing the fake window
above the sink. As I moved in past her toward the hot water tap, I noticed that she was removing bread from a sandwich she had purchased in the vending machine. Nora was
like a surgeon with that sandwich. Precise and focused. In
delicate, uniform strokes, she was now using a paper napkin to dab the mayonnaise off the orange cheese.

"Looks like it's going to be another sunny day," I said,
gesturing to the photo of the Swiss Alps printed on the
cardboard window. She didn't laugh. She didn't respond
in any sort of way. She simply kept dabbing, staring at the
American cheese.

"Jerry's looking for you," she finally said.

"I'm on my way to see him, after I make him this cup of coffee."

She looked at her cheese.

"Are you doing all right?" I asked.

She looked up. She looked back down. She must have heard me, but didn't seem to care. I sprinkled instant coffee into a mug of hot water. The flakes turned to blurry dashes, the dashes turned into dark spots that sought each other out, the brown consumed the clear: coffee.

She walked over to the small dining nook and sat down. She had her survey there. She must have been working on it during her snack break. I had to join her. I could not imagine not joining her. It was a bold move for me, considering how all her cheer made me talk dumb, and feel dumb. I sat down and casually took a sip of the coffee. The nook was cramped. My knees pressed against the bottom of the table. There was nothing in the cushion to keep me from feeling the cheap wood of the bench.

"I'm not sad," she said, holding on to her inner sandwich.

"I didn't say you were."

"You asked me if I was okay."

"Just curious."

"I am fine. I don't know. Maybe this survey"—it seemed like she wanted to say *fucking survey*—"has gotten under my skin."

I liked what she was saying. Her recognition of her dismay. I smiled. She didn't like that.

"Why am I talking to you? I don't even know you." She

said it, and then looked at me and must have detected some fraction of humanity in my face. "Oh gosh, I'm sorry. Why did I say that? Don't tell anybody I said that. It just slipped out. I like everybody. I really do."

"We belong to the same credit union."

"Huh?"

"You said you didn't know me."

"Right."

"But what were you saying about your skin?" I looked at her skin, freckled and athletic, slightly sun-damaged. I imagined biting the gold chain off of her neck and spitting it out. I wanted to put a finger to a freckle on her cheek and see if either of us could feel something from the inside of the other. I also wanted to read her survey, which helped me remember what I was going to say. "How has this gotten under your skin?"

She didn't answer.

I said, "I'll tell you about my feelings if you tell me about what's gotten under your skin."

There is an attitude children have, when they want to tell something important to their parent, but their parent isn't nearby, and you, the only adult around, offer to help, and the child tells you, reluctantly, what is on their mind, but they say it in such a way that makes clear that they see you as a substitute, and that telling you isn't going to satisfy their needs to the degree it might if you were their mommy or daddy. It was in this same way that Nora finally spoke to me. She said, and she seemed genuinely upset by it, "I work in Employee Regard. Obviously you know this."

"Uh-huh." My ass was getting sore on the lousy Winnebago bench.

"This self-appraisal thing should have come from Employee Regard. Right?"

I hadn't thought about it.

"Where else would it come from? But I *am* Regard, and I didn't know anything about it. Zilch."

I took another sip of Jerry's coffee and made a mental note to make the next cup stronger.

"Somebody's trying to steal my thunder," she went on, "with this fucking survey. It doesn't even make sense. Some of these questions don't make sense, unless they are some kind of mind trap. But it doesn't matter. Somebody came up with it, and it wasn't me." There was a territorial animal in that curly headed little acrobat. Her teeth looked sharper as she spoke. "Why didn't I think of it? All I ever thought up were karaoke parties in the parking lot and all that obvious holiday-themed bullshit. Foosball Thursdays. Banana split Wednesdays. Putting Jerry in a dunk tank. Over-the-top shit, heavy on razzle-dazzle and streamers, excuses for people to get boozed up a little. But now this fucking survey comes along. Whoever is behind this is going to out-kudos me. I want a promotion to Customer Acclaim. I always have. They get to travel to Dallas every year. I want that."

"But you are very good at what you do." Was she? Did I care? I imagined her in her teens, bouncing around on blue tumbling mats. I pictured her spinning in the air, a leotard clinging to her lean body, moist spots under her arms, her toenails painted with flags on them, her head of curls tamed by high-performance hair spray. Spinning like a competitive maniac and then landing perfectly and breaking the judges' hearts.

A tear fell onto the orange cheese. Apparently she really wanted to go to Dallas. I offered her a napkin in case she started to have a full cry. The napkin had a picture of a home on it. The home was smiling. She blew her nose right into the mouth.

I wanted to tell her the perfect reassuring thing, but I wasn't sure what that would be. So I told her about my sadness, figuring we were on the same side of the virus. I said, "Sometimes I close my eyes and I try to look deep inside my body; even though there is no real location for our feelings, I imagine they are housed somewhere in my thorax, and I picture dipping my hand in to get a look at them. But what I pull out are broken objects—pots, urns, plates, unidentifiable fragments. I look at them and I hold them and I have no idea what they were originally used for."

She took a bite of her breadless sandwich and made a sour face. She threw the rest in the trash. Then she said, "I have to get back to planning the travel barbecue launch party." Her indifference hurt, but then she handed me her survey, a minor consolation for being so aloof.

"Take this," she said, "and put it with the rest of the fucking surveys. I don't think I answered it correctly, but at some point I stopped caring." She paused and thought about what she'd said. "Don't tell anybody. Especially

Jerry. I know how word gets around. I said I stopped caring. But I care. I do." With a smile that looked practiced, she walked away, erect and spring-loaded.

If she was willing to stop caring, then I was willing to stop caring if anybody saw me reading her survey, which is what I did while drinking the rest of Jerry's coffee.

NAME: NORA PEPPERDINE

Are you single?

Yes. Though sometimes I feel married to the company. But not in a bad way.

Are you having an affair?

With this company. Hah. (That was a joke. I love it here.)

Are you who you want to be?

I am doing very well. As you probably know, I started as an intern, parking cars and working the espresso cart. I data-entried and now I events-coordinate. I love working in the Employee Regard department. I could work in this department for the rest of my life, though I do love new challenges and Customer Acclaim seems like a fun crowd too and a great challenge, should something open up there. I mean, the customer comes first, right?

Are you similar to the "you" you thought you would become when as a child you imagined your future self?

I thought I would be endorsing cereals and using my celebrity to help the United Way. But I have a great apartment near the freeway, which makes my commute a real cinch, and there is an on-site health club here at work and at my apartment building.

When was the last time you felt happy?

I am happy. I am, really, and when I am not happy, I just make myself happy. I buy a diet soda and listen to classic rock.

Was it a true, pure happy or a relative happy?

I would never be dishonest about my happy.

Do you realize you have on average another 11,000 to 18,250 mornings of looking in the mirror and wondering if people will find you attractive?

That's why I have a really big mirror with vanity bulbs.

Karl Flannigan walked into the break room. He was tall. Too tall for the Winnebago. Hunched over, he gave the vending machine a long stare, jingled his change in his hand deliberatively, and waved over at me without taking his gaze away from the machine.

I read more.

Do you believe in life after death?

Of course. I can't wait to meet Jesus. I hear he talks to you for as long as you want up there. He'll go on walks with you. He's just got a lot of time for communicating, and you can put your head on his shoulder, and he'll whisper you a joke, and it's totally appropriate, and it makes you feel better, even though you already feel great, because you are in heaven and heaven is number one.

Do you believe in life after God?

That is a sad thought. I hope God never dies. Who'll take care of us?

Are you for the chemical elimination of all things painful?

Only until the wound heals.

Do you think we need more sports?

Hard to say. There are some pretty great sports out there. Maybe a sport to include the larger people, because I feel like they don't appreciate sports, because they don't know how fun they can be, because

they are larger, so they think sports are
stupid, but they aren't. Is it bad to say
that? I don't think anybody here is too
large, and even if I did, I think that's
great. I was just talking about sports is
all. For sports it can be a problem. I
love all people. I'm not perfect either.

Have you ever fallen in love?

I love my dad. I loved my coach, but that
got us into trouble. I love somebody else
right now, and I think he loves me, but he
isn't able to give me everything. But he
will by this spring vacation, which I
planned for us. So the answer is yes.

I wasn't sure what to make of her survey. I don't think she is happy. I don't believe her. She wants to go to Dallas. That in itself is a sign that something is askew. But the bulk of her answers were corrupted by the context of the survey. She was looking at it like an exam rather than a chance to get to know her malady.

I folded Nora's survey so Karl couldn't see what I was reading, and went back to the counter to create a new cup of coffee for Jerry. Karl was heating something in the toaster oven and tapping his finger to an internal rhythm.

I said, "Whatcha heating, Karl?"

"An Asian breakfast burrito."

"Smells good." It didn't.

Do you hear voices?

Dead people. Little versions of me bundled in rope, struggling to formulate sentences. Sometimes the trees and clouds.

Lorraine LaFevre, Jerry's assistant, was on the phone, and it didn't sound like business. "And then what? . . . Uh-huh . . . Well, I wouldn't take that . . . You know he wouldn't get away with saying that kind of junk to me . . . Yeah, but he doesn't know it isn't his . . . No, you didn't! . . . You did? . . . Oh my." Her hair was formatted with chemicals into the shape of a swirling shrub.

She held her hand over the phone, protecting her personal conversation, and said, "Is Jerry expecting you?"

"He said ASAP, and"—I motioned to the mug in my hand—"I brought him coffee."

"Mary, I'll have to call you back."

I stood and waited.

"Why don't you take a seat?"

A little coffee spilled onto my hand as I lowered myself into one of the five beanbags in the waiting area. The beanbags looked like the deflated eggs of a two-hundred-foot salmon. We were pushing the items in our summer catalogs. There was a tendency to promote inside the company whatever new products we were hustling on the outside, to cultivate an enthusiasm from within. Sitting lopsided on an orange pink sack was not cultivating an enthusiasm from within.

Lorraine opened the door into Jerry's office and stuck her head in while keeping the rest of her body in the reception area. She was wearing a blue skirt. Her calves looked like bowling pins.

She came back to her desk and told me Jerry was expecting me.

I said, "How are you feeling today?"

"Busy." She started clicking on her mouse and staring at her screen.

I said, "Would you like to help me get out of this beanbag?"

She raised one eyebrow. That was all the response I got.

Jerry had a corner office. Square. The two halves that made the corner were all window. It looked onto the imitation brook that ran through the campus. He was at his desk listening to space shuttle music. It was a composition designed to keep astronauts motivated as they tightened bolts on satellites. Without the music, according to the liner notes, the space workers were more likely to drift off into prolonged dream states. Jerry had told me once that it increased his efficiency and at the end of the same conversation offered to sell me a copy at cost.

"Just one second, bud." He was fiddling with a phone tablet thing, organizing his communicating. I set the coffee down next to him, trying not to distract him.

A bird flew into one of the windows and crashed to the ground outside.

"Fucking birds," said Jerry, without looking up from his gadget. "Don't they get that it's glass?"

I was on the bird's side. I happen to love birds. They have small hearts. They have song. They can scream when they are in their cages, alone with the child of the house; scream when they smell fire and tell the child to get the fuck out. And they have a delicately wound biological mechanism within them, like an elaborate clock made out of miniature bones, or so I imagine it, that allows them to fly up and down the globe without getting lost.

I waited in a chair across from Jerry. I watched him. Forgetting about the bird's death as soon as it happened, he was hunched over, tapping at his device, unhappy with the information it was relaying back to him. I looked at his huge forehead. There was room on it for a second face. I started to draw his forehead's face on a piece of paper while I waited for him. This second face was looking down at the first face wondering when the first face would stop tinkering with the gadget.

"Sorry about this, Ray," he said, gesturing to the device, "but it's ten minutes before race time, and I'm just trying to breathe a little air into the revenue growth of one of our Latin operations."

I started to feel a hiss at the base of my jaw. Jerry always spoke in an unintelligible business vernacular, but this was the first time I could recall the words triggering a physical reaction in my body.

"Ouch," I said. Not to Jerry, but because my jaw hurt.

"Fair enough. Fair enough, Ray. You're absolutely right. I shouldn't be wasting your time, what with the secret little project you have going on."

My head followed this approximate line of thought: The survey. Bob Grasston. Sauna. Project incomplete. Shit. Snitched on. Fired. Problems. Mad Brenda. Brenda leave me. Feelings? Hug Don. Kiss Nora. Fight Charlie. Confess? Whimper? Flee. Correction: Take pens from supply closet, then flee.

"Secret project?" I said.

"Bob Grasston told me. I think he's jealous."

"One of his graphs?"

"Ray, stop being coy. I haven't time to beat around the bush. I have things to implement. Wars to wage. Armies to creep up on in the night, and one of them is in Bangalore of all places."

Jerry was fond of using military metaphors to describe our work. He always asked Don and me how things were down in the trenches. Once, while firing somebody, he likened the man's dismissal to amputating a soldier's gangrenous leg.

"Would you like a drink?"

"Is that allowed?"

"It is if I offer you one."

"Are you having one?"

He got out some highball glasses with bright pink *L*s on them and filled them with something whiskey-colored.

"You should have checked with me first, Ray. There are legal steps we could have taken. If people had signed releases, we could have had a lot more flexibility with this data. Some of these questions aren't very professional."

"I thought all the surveys were on my desk?"

"Come on, Ray. These things spread. You know that. Somebody asked me about the survey, and I said I'd never heard of such a thing, and could he forward the e-mail, and he said there was no e-mail. No e-mail? Smells fishy is what I thought."

I couldn't respond.

"No offense, and credit where credit is due," he continued, "but I'm going to hire a firm to do this right. The whole gamut. Quizzes. Puzzles. Ink-blob free association. Polygraphs. I don't care what it takes."

He was looking at me like he was making music just for me. He kept talking in weird patterns that went up and down and curled around themselves like roller coasters. I stopped listening to the words themselves and instead tried to figure out what shapes the words might have. Very odd shapes. Chocolate shapes. Strawberry shapes. Barnacle shapes.

He sipped on his drink. I pretended to sip on mine.

He kept talking. He said what I did takes balls. He said he likes balls, though not in those very words. He talked about growing up in these buildings, living his life here, having a feel for the job, seeing a lot of things—beautiful things, horrific things—fighting a lot of fights, sleeping under the stars, eating grubs off the jungle floor, pulling himself up by his bootstraps, carrying wounded men miles, pulling the pins out of hand grenades, crying in tidal waves when one of his men went down, flying a chopper with both arms in a sling. The whole speech, slippery as it was, had an end in sight that somehow pertained to me. That was clear.

At the very first opening I said, "I've been thinking of taking a leave of absence." I was surprised that saying it didn't surprise me. I knew that on some level the job was killing me, but I also knew that leaving the job would cause Brenda to kill me.

Jerry had an awkward swallow that transitioned into a misshapen laugh.

"I see what you are doing," he said. "You're trying to gain a little leverage. I like it, but don't push it. A man like me likes to feel charitable, not cornered. We get cornered, we lose our charity."

"I'm afraid I don't follow."

"Back to the coy games, I see. Raymond, what do you want? I'll pay you double—well, not double, but more than you make now. You can have your own apartment here on campus. I'll make Nora your personal assistant. How does that sound?"

I began to speak, but he said, "Shh. Let's drink a little first. You need to let this sink in."

He poured the remainder of the liquor into his glass. Looking at the empty state of the decanter, he said, "This won't do," and started riffling through his drawers, and then searched his coat closet.

"Ray, what do you have to do? Can you hold on while I get another bottle?"

"I was going to finish up the proofs for the LCD mailboxes."

"Nonsense."

He rushed out. I could hear him in the waiting room saying something to Lorraine.

I walked over to the corner of his office, where the windows meet, to pour out the remainder of my whiskey into a potted palm. Looking out the windows I saw traffic buzzing along, the shine of identical buildings, a current of energy that looked habitual rather than purposeful. I saw the bird on the ground, its neck broken. Poor fellow. It had tried to kiss its reflection and that was its crime. Little drops of bird blood splattered at the beak. Dying eyes looking for an explanation.

Turning around to head back to my seat before Jerry got back, I spied a survey on his desk. Could it be? Could this man honestly deny his sadness in the face of my questions? Was it accurate to call him a man? Did he even know what feelings were? I grabbed it and rushed back to my seat. I began to fold it, to conceal it, but then I quickly began reading instead, because I could not help myself.

Are you single?

```
I am married to Gayle Samberson, the
mother of my children.
```

Would you prefer to be someone else?

   If I had an identical twin, I would
   consume him to be even more like myself.

**Are you similar to the "you" you thought
you would become when as a child you
imagined your future self?**

   I imagined this very nameplate that sits
   on my desk when I was thirteen. I didn't
   have the title down, but I could see my
   name inset in white letters.

I heard something outside. I sat on the survey and
pretended to be doing nothing. I waited. I was still. I
looked at the walls. A photo of Jerry cutting a ribbon in
front of a commercial outlet. Next to the photo was a map
of the world with the names of countries replaced by the
names of our biggest-selling products. The continents
were pink and the oceans were green. Iceland was as big
as Africa.

Nobody came in, so I read some more.

**Do you think people will remember you
after you die?**

   I doubt that I will die anytime soon.

For how long after you die?

   How long does a bronze statue stand erect
   in a corporate garden?

Do you believe in life after death?

> I will recline on a cloud and look down on
> all of the work I have accomplished in my
> life. An angel will hand me a telescope to
> witness my legacies. I will smoke a cigar.
> You can't get cancer in heaven, either
> because they have cancer-free cigar
> technology or more likely because you
> aren't technically alive.

Are you for the chemical elimination of
all things painful?

> If we could secure manufacturing rights.

Do you think we need more sports?

> I think we may need more sports-related
> furniture.

I heard Jerry talking to Lorraine again. I folded and
stuffed the survey into my pocket and swirled my glass
around and started whistling to myself. Jerry entered and
noticed my empty glass.

"Good man! Not to worry. Reinforcements have arrived," he said, waving a full bottle. "I'm glad you are un-
winding, Raymond. Very glad. You know, I was quite
enjoying our talk. We all work so much, sometimes we
need these little rap sessions."

Jerry's friendliness made me uncomfortable. He was
acting like he trusted me. Like he was going to give me the

keys to his kingdom. A friendly overture from the school bully. I didn't want to step over to his side, nor did I fully trust the gesture, but the protection had some allure. But then as I considered the allure, I could feel something inside of me shrinking, or preparing to shrink. Some aspect of myself.

"Are you married, Raymond?" He poured himself some more. He poured me some more. I pretended to take a sip. I made a sound I imagined I would make if I were enjoying it, an appreciative sigh.

"Yes, I am. I believe you met my wife at one of the Christmas parties. Brenda. Dark hair. Glasses. Sharp wit." I could tell he wasn't listening. His eyes were somewhere else.

"Yes, yes. Nice work. Lovely woman," he said, and then, "What about something on the side?"

"Excuse me?"

He paused, wondering perhaps if I was truly a member of his platoon.

"You are accepting the promotion, correct?" he said.

"I suppose so," I said. I felt cold. I was shivering somewhere just under the skin.

"You suppose so?"

"How could I not?" I started to think about fire exits. Where the nearest one was. I began to miss the interior of my car. I began to miss my wife, or at least the time when I used to miss my wife. I thought about my childhood: soft foods, familiar blankets, bath toys I missed deeply.

"Some of your questions in this survey got me thinking

about the past. Certain indiscretions. Things I haven't told people. Things I shouldn't tell people. Things people could use against me."

"I think it is the things we use against ourselves that are the real killers." It sounded like nonsense as I said it, but I tried to relax anyway. Let go a little. Enjoy the discomfort of our exchange as best I could. I thought about our thoughts—my thoughts, Jerry's thoughts, everybody's thoughts—swirling around in outer space, an astro-cloud of ideas and emotions, a celestial storm light-years away, and our bodies acting as receivers. We were like radios sitting next to each other, picking up programming that wasn't necessarily related, simulating a conversation, because our bodies were in a close proximity, and sounds were coming out, and at times our meanings intersected, if only slightly.

He walked from his desk over to the love seat, which was closer to the leather chair I was sitting in. A conversation pit, minus the pit, made of sample furniture. We were much closer now. Direct eye contact was difficult to avoid.

"Do you remember Debbie Rayburn?"

"Vaguely."

"She worked as my assistant. In Lorraine's position. Real sharp dresser. Loved the color cyan."

"That sort of rings a bell." In my memory all of his assistants blended together into one big mound of makeup and overburdened hair arrangements.

"Well, she had a mole on her upper lip. The kind that drives a man wild. It wasn't something I could control.

Which was liberating in a way—to have no choice but to yield to the urge and pounce."

"Like an animal?"

"Like a savage," he said, with the glee of a child deciding on the ideal Halloween costume.

"Do you think savages are aware of their own existence—I mean, in a historical sense?" I was hoping this might take the conversation in a more philosophical direction.

He stared at me like I was eating salad with the wrong fork. A large forehead of disappointment.

"Well, back to Debbie." As he said it he reached over his shoulder to the bookshelf that was behind his chair and grabbed a stuffed pink and green giraffe. He found it almost without looking. Like the way a championship quarterback knows ahead of time the precise location where his all-star receiver will end his route before hurling the ball downfield. A muscle memory perfected through practice. The giraffe was one of our more popular children's toys. It had been resting on the shelf as a bookend to some business titles—*The Joy of Business*, *Alpha Manager*, *Will to Consume*. He held the stuffed animal against his chest and relaxed deeply. "It took months to crack her. I started out subtle. I talked about my sore shoulders, how they were stiff; I talked about the stress of work, how I simply needed a release of some sort or another."

He sipped on his whiskey, looking past me, up to the ceiling, slinking lower in the love seat. "Eventually I switched tacks, became more direct, told her how incredibly attractive she was. The things I said became more and more suggestive, descriptive, anatomical."

Now I took a real sip of my whiskey.

"But she resisted. Avoided me. She was always in a region of my office that I wasn't." I imagined him—his big head, his strong grip, his large knuckled hands, his project-management eyes—chasing after the poor woman. "Just as I was nearing my body toward hers or putting my hand around her hand, which was around a pencil," he said, "she would slip out of reach."

The last comment reminded him of a fishing story. A slippery fish flopping around in a bucket. A chartered cruise in the Arab Emirates. Advice on treating sunburn he learned from a man named Ahmed. He took me along for the entire detour, and then finally got back to his original thread. "And then once she didn't really resist, and slowly it became a regular thing."

Jerry was almost lying down in the chair. His legs were splayed far out, wide open; most of his back was on the seat; his hands were resting on his thighs; his head was looking upward in a trance state, lost in confession. The giraffe was napping on his chest, rising and falling along with Jerry's breath.

"Was it what I wanted?" he went on rhetorically. "In some ways, maybe. The first time was thrilling. There is no disputing that. Animal, erotic, bordering on illegal. Just tremendous. But it never got back to that, no matter the risk of the locale. We did it in the parking lot. In the conference rooms. We probably did it on your desk. On every desk in the building, while the Guatemalans cleaned the place at night. But it was never as incredible as that first time."

He kept talking, and I could tell he didn't want to be interrupted. But my radio was still receiving signals too. I was contemplating injuring myself. Trying to think of a painless way to make my arms not work for some temporary period of time. Fantasizing about a paid leave; of afternoons in a library, researching various theories about the collective emotional framework of humanity, which was something I thought I believed in. All of us part of a larger organism. We were all together in this. Except then I looked at Jerry talking on and on—comparing his sex with Debbie to an army that had forgotten why it was fighting, then getting off course and sharing with me a trick for getting lightbulbs to last longer, and what it felt like the first time he killed a deer, and why rainstorms made him think of a pet turtle he had in his youth.

I looked at the clock as he said all of this. It didn't have any numbers on it. Every hour was an illustration of a piece of furniture. It was currently an end table past a lamp.

"And so the answer to that is no," he said, to a question I hadn't heard.

Because he wasn't looking, or maybe as an act of defiance, I pulled out his survey for something to read while he went on. Maybe I even wanted to get caught, to break his trust, to disband this alliance.

Have you ever fallen in love?

    Gayle. She was my nurse. We met when I had
    plantar warts removed. The way she so

delicately applied dry ice to the warts
and then scraped away the dead growth
broke my heart.

**If yes, were you surprised that it, like
all other things, faded over time?**

Our love will outlive the tides.

I read that while he said, "I was making love to Debbie
on a big pile of those imitation bearskin rugs that were
such big sellers a few years ago, and I was having the
toughest time finishing, if you know what I mean. So I
imagined someone else. Pictured somebody else in my
mind." He gave me a moment to contemplate what he was
saying. "And do you think you can guess who that was?"

I couldn't.

"I imagined my wife. I imagined that it was my wife
who I was making love to, but in Debbie's irresistible pant-
suit."

He looked wistful and faraway. I felt like I was visiting
with someone who had dementia. They start to inhabit an
older part of their brain that still feels alive, and it doesn't
really involve you—they are talking to the ice man, recov-
ering old private memories, horses are still a popular
means of transport, paperboys wear those funny caps—
and you don't really know when or if they are going to
come back to the present, and you can't quite decide
whether it is more polite to stay or leave.

He kept talking about his "termination." Its brilliance.
He made it sound like an epic battle with bows and arrows

and cannonballs and slaves and lions and Romans. He was holding the giraffe again, close to his heart. I was looking at his survey.

Do you realize you have on average another 11,000 to 18,250 mornings of looking in the mirror and wondering if people will find you attractive?

I don't look in the mirror in the morning. Gayle combs my hair for me. I read the paper while she does this.

"As soon as I could, I rushed home to my wife. I had to have her. It was all I could think about. She was busy playing solitaire on her laptop. I kissed her on her neck. I tried to put my hands through her hair, but it was in a bun and I didn't know how to maneuver around that. She was a little irritated. Said she was in the middle of a good hand. I explained to her my needs. My urges. Reminded her she could save her game by pressing 'command S.'" He looked proud as he said it. "And so we walked up the stairs to the bedroom. And I even lit candles—you know, the ones we sell that look like fish jumping out of streams—and we made love. And it was terrible. Like eating stale crackers, reading a soggy newspaper. Not one thrill. And then we lay there, and my wife wept. And I missed being in my office. I was overwhelmed by a deep desire to check my e-mail."

And he told me that little had changed in his marriage,

and he accepted that, and he said the next year he was an even more efficient worker than in the previous one, and he doubled the length of his goals, and tripled the rate of achieving his goals, and now they are flying him to Iceland to receive an award soon, and his youngest son is becoming quite a little shortstop on his baseball team, and the other one not a bad trombonist, and LokiLoki sold four million travel sofas last year, and 1.2 billion plastic beer glasses, and that he hasn't missed a day of work in five years, and that he reads at least one success biography a month, and that he just got a physical and the doctor told him he had the heart of a twenty-year-old, and then he finally looped around to his earlier theme and said, "Even now when I get together with Debbie, and we make love, I always imagine it's my wife, and that usually does the trick, and if that doesn't work, I think about checking my e-mail, and that definitely does the trick, and I can't for the life of me make any sense of this routine, so I don't."

He looked up, looked around, confirmed his surroundings after such an intense departure. He was like one of those séance ladies who jabbers the voices of the dead for their remaining relatives and then reenters her own body, her regular consciousness returning to the room—looking around as if to say, *Did anything shake up while I was out of body?* That is what it was like. Jerry saw me. He knew he had been relating private details. He took note of the survey in my hands. He saw that I had been reading it. And I thought, *There isn't anything in here that is as bad as what he just told me.* But he looked betrayed. So what I did was I let the radio transmissions direct me for a bit. I kind of waved out. In a half-present, or maybe doubly present state, I walked over and took the giraffe out of his hands, and then I returned to my seat, and I held the giraffe, and I began to talk to him—the giraffe—and to Jerry, and let them listen to my transmissions.

I said, "Jerry, we were never meant to be here. We were never meant to be us." I petted the giraffe on the head as I said it. Other than the colors, it really was a nice little toy. "We're a mistake. We are growing and getting bigger, but we are still a mistake. Everything we strive for, a mistake. We don't work right. We're all very sick. Very, very sick. And we're eating our own shit, lapping it up, as fast as we can, which is naturally making us even sicker. And as I say this I feel very certain that we'll die off soon. Much sooner than later. We're like horses with wings who are too fat to fly. Beautiful horses. Beautiful wings. An incredible combination. A miracle of evolution. But way too fat to fly." I looked over at him and he seemed a little threatened. Like a kid who doesn't like the rules of the game, or didn't mind the rules while he was winning but is definitely looking to disrupt the rules now that the lead is changing. "If you understand even a whit of what I am saying, can you then see how working here is like building things specifically for landfills? Sure, our initial customers are poor people, not landfills—and by *poor* I don't mean economically disadvantaged so much as simply defenseless against our advances. But these aren't our real customers. Our real customer is a festering hole in the earth, and we are cramming our cheap furniture down its throat like it is a duck and we are trying to make pâté."

I looked over at Jerry. He stood up. He was walking over to me. I wondered if he was the kind of drunk who likes to fight or the kind who likes to hug. He stared down at me. His face was red. He couldn't figure me out. I was a product that was impossible to assemble.

Do you realize you have on average another 11,000 to 18,250 mornings of looking in the mirror and wondering if people will find you attractive?

I sit in front of the mirror for what feels like hours but is probably never longer than three minutes. I stretch my face. I pull down on my cheeks, which stretches my lower eyelids down so that you can see the pink icky part bordering the lower eyeball, and I talk in accents that I imagine to be authentic to people who can't read—people I call gun owners. I will talk about marrying my cousin or eating squirrel brains or running over children with the big tractor wheels on my raised-up truck. Idiotic, bigoted things that I say with deep concentration to my manipulated reflection. I do this, and enjoy it quite a bit, and then I realize I am talking to myself, and I get on with dressing and eating breakfast and going over the to-do list that Brenda has made for me.

As I walked back to my desk the light in the building turned in on itself. It was probably in part the whiskey and in even bigger part the residue of channeling the far-off broadcasts. It doesn't make any sense, but that is how it was. Blues turned to orange. Black became white. Red became green. My coworkers moved in slow motion. Polaroid negatives of busy people. There was no sound. I looked in a cubicle and Ron Turner was pointing to some pornography on his computer and Ted Jenkins was in there and they were laughing like it was a clever joke, holding their quaking ribs and laughing, like there was real wit involved in sticking a thirty-nine-dollar camera up to a contorted labia. They saw me walking by, and they both gave me an aw-shucks look as if to say, "This sought us out, not the other way around."

I felt sideways. Upturned. I passed a conference room. One of the less formal ones, for sit-down chats, where supervisors practice listening techniques. The couches were plump and unused, overstuffed and injected with neon dyes to make them look more playful. Rita Carlyle was on one, submerged in personal conversation, whispering into the phone. I read her lips: "I hate my job . . . I miss you . . . People are stupid . . . I've already had four energy drinks so far today . . . I hate my new phone . . . Why are postage stamps so expensive?"

Walking on in the silence of our communal rot, I composed a letter in my head:

Dear Mr. President,

There is no reason to believe you will read this. You are probably in the middle of important plastic surgery with the Joint Chiefs of Staff. But there is an emergency. *We* are the emergency. I don't know if all the simple humans fucking and shitting and farming and texting all over this spinning earth can look up all at once and say together, in a grand chorus of self-awareness, "We are not well," but I think it will take something like that. Can I prove it? I suspect I could, with a little help from our nation's top scientists. Will tackling this problem advance your career? I don't know, but you are already president—how much further do you need to advance?

I passed the printer where my survey had first been exposed. The intern from the Bible college was standing there trying to fix a jammed stapler. He smiled at me. I looked the other way.

At my desk I wrote a rough draft of the letter to the president as quickly as I could. While typing, the common-sense side of my head was saying, *This is a waste of time.* But writing the draft, protecting the thoughts before they slipped away, made me feel good. I sent it to a personal e-mail account that I could access away from the office, be-cause I knew I wouldn't be coming back.

I took a deep breath. The colors returned to normal. I could hear again. The sound of a thousand microchips fan-ning themselves. The slow electric bleed of processors. I collected my favorite pens, stuffing them in my pockets and, when there wasn't enough room, putting even more of them into a cardboard box. I looked around my desk for more. There was a trophy I had won for "Excellence in Output." I threw it in the trash can. There was a framed photo of Brenda from right after our honeymoon. It had been hidden behind the now discarded trophy and a gift-size jar of pretzels. Brenda was pretty in the photograph. That's probably why it was hidden back there. The forgot-ten Brenda. An easy smile and sympathetic eyes that could make me talk. It was not long after I took the photo that I landed the promising job of Assistant Pictographer. I re-member it made Brenda happy. I had interviewed and we waited every day for a week to hear if they would hire me. Making Brenda happy made me happy. I felt like some-body. I would have health coverage. An occupation. Some-thing easier to explain to people than my noncareer as a fine artist, oil paintings from photographs I had taken at the morgue. I felt safe with the job. A protection from poverty and insanity. I wouldn't become the man who sits in conversation with himself at the public library. I was gaining citizenship to a powerful country with a solid infrastructure and significant defense budget. I remember telling her, after getting the offer on the phone, "They really do make some nifty things. Practical things. Things you can sit on." She squeezed my arm and we looked through a catalog, picking out a lamp and an end table that we would buy at the employee rate, and then we probably rolled around on top of each other and, when we got tired of that, had food delivered to our apartment and ate it in bathrobes.

I put the picture of Brenda in a shoebox. Then I slowly took the photographs down from my cubicle walls, leaving behind brighter pink rectangles where the fabric hadn't faded or collected dust. An albino man serving hot dogs in an amusement park. A dwarfish girl in a full-body cast holding on to a bouquet of balloons with her one good hand. A woman in a nursing uniform with feline eyeglasses bottle-feeding an infant chimpanzee. And the child soldier. He gave me the same cold stare. I wanted him to know that I would fight too. I would publicly humiliate those who had wronged him and his family. I touched a finger to my lips and then I pressed it to his. He still looked back at me like my life had no value.

Why are you so sad?

Because there is a swell of pain inside me, and it is beginning to compromise the structural integrity of my emotional skeleton. Because hope feels like something that was discontinued due to safety concerns. Because I can't make love to the billboards but am compelled to try anyway. Because when I wake up I resent that I have to go on living. Because when I try to tell people how I feel, they say, "That reminds me of a very funny television commercial I just saw." Because everything I touch—the ottoman, the remote, the shoes, the coffee table, the collectible flatware, the books, the friendships, the interior of my car, the clothing, the records, my wife, the CDs (and the crappy plastic cases they come in), the old letters from friends I met at summer camp thirty years ago, the pocketknife that belonged to my grandfather, the flowers I cut and put in water, the finger paintings the slow kid that lives next door gave to me, the houseplants, the sunsets, the secrets I am afraid to share, the angry letters to my congressperson, the children I will never have, my marriage, my job, everything and every other thing—fades or crumbles into broken parts that I can never reassemble.

She handed me her card: Doreese Cummings, Associate Facilitator, Human Resources. Her cubicle had multiple Kleenex boxes at the ready and a calendar with photos of athletes in wheelchairs. There were other framed photos on her desk of people I assumed were important to her. A boy with carefully combed hair and her same porcine nose. Another man in vacation clothing with his arm around her.

"I'll be your point person while you are away," she said. She smelled like the world's cleanest closet, with brand-new carpet and potpourri bundles hanging down.

I said, "Doreese, it is very nice to meet you, but I am not sure I need your help."

I had no intention of hurting her feelings, but I also didn't feel like humoring her. She couldn't help me. She was no less sick than any of us. If she couldn't address her own illness, how could she help me with mine? And with every passing moment since Jerry and I shared the giraffe, it was becoming more impossible to imagine a return to this place. I was a Senior Pictographer no more. In my mind I saw a computer monitor, with its evil glow, opened to the frustrating illustration software I was forced to use. The inked quill icon was drawing Mr. CustomMirth®, and he was miming an elaborate farewell speech; his fat, fingerless mitten hands were wishing me well, telling me it was time to move on, that he'd be fine, that he'd miss me, and that nobody else could give him a soul while still keeping him customer-appropriate, but who the fuck cares? For this last part, he stuck out his tongue and made an elaborate gesture with his forearm to imply an empowering, nonconsensual sexual act involving the corporation's anus. His point was: The world was crumbling. If you're a crew member on a sinking ship, do you continue to swab the decks once you confirm that the ship is, in fact, sinking? Why would you? Of course, I had no idea what was next for me, which was thrilling but also mildly horrifying. Just imagining Brenda's pending tirade made my stomach feel like sour milk and broken glass. Still, at least I was being honest. The one human being trying to be honest. The ship was sinking. I would not go down quietly. I either had to solve the problem or prepare for a life underwater.

Doreese gave me a nod that seemed to suggest only people who need help say they don't think they need help.

"Let's start here," she said, and handed me a brochure for a service called TheraRestore by Phone. "For many people TheraRestore is the first step toward a rejuvenating sabbatical."

I looked at the brochure. It had a photo of a woman smiling, talking into a phone like the phone was a little baby she wanted to kiss and tickle. She was pretty, with dynamic eyelashes, and her red mouth was so close to the phone it looked like she was going to smudge the receiver with lipstick. The brochure made being crazy and talking to somebody about being crazy seem sexy. I tried to imagine having a conversation with a real teletherapist. Not the woman in the photo; I knew better than to believe in her. But a pool of part-time mothers, working in cubicles just like my cubicle, but in India, breast-feeding their children or doing their nails while looking through magazines.

"Many employees have found a lot of peace through TheraRestore, and LokiLoki is prepared to pay up to three quarters of the cost, not including prescriptions," Doreese told me.

Perhaps sensing I wasn't sold on phone therapy, she said, "Nobody's perfect," as if the information was new to me, and would then help me feel less alone in my imperfections. She thought I was crazy. But I wasn't crazy. Being aware of a deep hurting inside all of us isn't crazy. Not being able to not hear things is not crazy.

"That's why we make our gods perfect," I said, because I understood, especially in moments like this, the severe longing for a flawless father or mother hovering up in the clouds, with some authoritative, parentlike explanation for what otherwise felt like an intentionless heap of stinking chaos below.

I said it and then I looked at the lapel of her power suit

and noticed she was wearing a button that said "God made me."

I felt bad that I might have offended her. Then I felt mad for having to feel bad. And then I felt bad for feeling mad. It wasn't her fault that they had her peddling these services. It wasn't her fault that God made her. And yet I wanted to unsettle her. Because I was feeling indignant, being thought of as crazy. I was the lucid one. I was. I could see inside of her—right past her cardigan, through her rayon blouse, into her core. She had a blind and innocent heart that was protected in layers of fat. She adored her filing systems. She loved her family. She pitied me. I greatly resented the pity.

I said, "Doreese, in the interest of reciprocity, why don't you fill out one of these emotional well-being self-appraisal forms for me?" I still had some. I had lied and said I would give Lorraine all the surveys in my possession before leaving the premises. Instead I gave her a stack of instructions on how to assemble a bumper pool table.

"We have a lot of paperwork to go through," she said. "Maybe afterward we can look at your questionnaire." Now she was being condescending. I could tell she looked down on questionnaires by the way she said it, as if she had some other preferred methodology. It made me want to antagonize her and her small, concerned mouth, and the photos on her desk of people who were probably good and kind. But then I also wanted to hold her, because it seemed that we all had big holes in our sides and really good things were slipping out, and that later the holes would heal into scars and the really good things would no longer be able to get back in.

I said, "Lorraine, you don't think I am coming back, do you?"

"My name's Doreese."

"I'm sorry."

"That's okay."

Her eyes were like marbles. I had collected marbles as a child. Some of my best memories are with marbles. I had marbles made of blown glass. I had ceramic marbles with beautiful cracked blue glazes.

Resisting the urge to touch her eyes, I said, "I think I am ready to go home now."

"Let me just put together the rest of your Leave Packet." She turned around to consult several pink and green binders.

I helped myself to some complimentary mints on her desk. A part of me wanted to stay and give her a chance to do her job so that she could feel good about herself, but that part of me didn't win out.

Do you believe in God?

I waver. If there is a God, he or she is sadistic or bored. It is possible that God is depressed. I probably would be. Look at what a bad job he or she is doing. Everything falls apart or gets cancer. He or she makes lots of beautiful little things, and then he or she makes bigger things that destroy the littler things. People, for instance: Some would argue they are God's finest achievement, but they have spun out of control, killing the lovely coral reefs and feeding the bees foods that are too perfectly shaped to digest. Bees cannot eat perfect hexagons. God knew this, but God did not think that he or she needed to tell people this, because people aren't God. But when people started to think they were God, it didn't work out so well. That was their edge, and their demise—thinking they could have a swing at being God, all the while praying to God, because this desire to be God was a little scary or didn't feel right, probably felt presumptuous, or maybe they just wanted to hedge their bets. But this edge, this inventiveness that was inventive in the image of God's inventiveness, screwed a lot of shit up, like feeding bees hexagons or engineering flowers that smelled like bacon. If God is so great and perfect, why did he or she go and make something as messy and hopelessly self-destructive as people? Which is why I mostly think there is no God, and we are merely a brief flash of energy that will be heard at the other side of the universe as the sound *phhhhssh-hpphhssshhppphhht*.

I had to cross that frightful expressway again to get to my car. I was carrying the artifacts of my career in a cardboard box: the surveys, a favorite mug, photos, some decent pens, HR forms. The traffic was no less aggressive than earlier that morning. If anything, it was more hostile. But my senses were heightened. I could not only see the approaching cars; I could hear inside of them. The sound of clenched hands tightly gripping steering wheels. The crushed breath mints. The banal chatter of minds searching for distraction. This elevated lucidity made me want to experiment. See if I could slip in between the seams without really looking. Return to my instincts. Sniff out the gaps in the flood of machinery. Which I did. I put one foot into the road, eyes closed, and began to move forward.

There was a thought, and there were the screams of cars. I experienced both concurrently. The thought that dangled up above my body was, *Maybe this is a bad idea*. A wall of air decorated in shrill horns pushed me back to the curb without killing me. My clarity was, I'll admit, a bit shaken. I felt the rage of the drivers. Blaming me for putting them in a position to kill me. Or maybe for almost making them late for dinner. I felt the honks. The middle fingers. The inevitable accusations. *A crazy man in the road.* They might have thought that. A man without a job. A man holding a box filled with personal research. Who knows what they saw? I couldn't hear inside of their cars anymore. The clarity comes, the clarity goes.

I tried crossing again, this time with my eyes open. The pavement was hot from a long day of rolling tires and exhaust. The sun was lowering at a glaring angle to my right, getting ready to make the evening pollution look like a gorgeous mistake. And the roadway was no less abominable. It was a dangerous dash, awkward from carrying the box; my ankles felt wobbly, but we did it. Reaching the median brought a familiar and welcome pause, though it was still loud as hell. I figured since I was there again, I might as well take a moment and see if I couldn't find the photo of the frog and finally introduce it to the other photos that were now in a folder in my cardboard box of personal items. And I did want to find that frog; I was sad that it had hopped away. But truthfully, more than the frog, I wanted to look at that flower again. Reconfirm its beauty. Take comfort. It was like an anchor. Here we are, all of us, afloat, facing something too large to understand, but the flower remains a flower. It doesn't matter what large thing it is you are facing. I was facing the burden of awareness. But it could be something else. You may be dying slowly in a nursing home. A man you've never seen before, who the nurse informs you is your son, regularly sends you flowers. You know life will end and absolutely none of the nagging riddles will be answered. Were you meant to marry? Were you meant to divorce? Were you a good person? Does this man, this son, send the flowers out of love, or guilt? Or is it perhaps an excuse to flirt regularly with a florist? Is the afterlife a metaphor for adulthood or senility? Why are some people so poor? Why are others born without limbs? Every question you ask has no answer, but the flower remains beautiful. It is not an answer. You know this. That it is beautiful proves nothing. It is a purely random coincidence. But that doesn't keep you from smiling when it arrives and the nurse puts it on the impersonal nightstand next to your folding bed. It's like when the grandchild says something funny without knowing why it's funny. The flower is just a beautiful series of combinations within a longer, less beautiful series. The longer series ripples on in endless variations. Some variations add up to the Holocaust. And some variations add up to wetting our bed until we are twelve. And some variations add up to the Crab Nebula. A flower is a nebula. Its color and shape are the most spectacularly beautiful nonanswer.

I set down my box for a moment and looked in the same weeds where I thought I had seen the flower before. I looked by other weeds that I thought were not the original weeds. I looked under a flyer for two free extra-large Cokes with any purchase of two extra-large pizzas. I looked under a torn and discarded baby bib. I looked uncomfortably close to a mound of animal excrement. I looked next to a perfectly good running shoe. I looked up to the sky. I raised my fist in contempt. But then I looked down again, and there by my feet were three of them. Not one—three. Like before: fat little petals, yellow yoke edged in blood. All three essentially the same: brilliant, sad, leaning, struggling, unknowing. Each one the same story, but not at all the same.

Do you think we need more sports?

I think we should unify all sports into one and call it Ultimate Tango.

PART TWO

MULTIPLE CHOICE

S chlitzy's Haus was not big on lighting. The food came smothered in shadows. The walls were covered in shingles and the shingles were covered in dirt. I was at the far end of a long beer hall table, sitting with my stack of surveys. My thought at that moment was, *What if I have one to five pints of beer before I get on to the business of alerting the world to the pending epidemic?*

I had stopped in on my drive home because I didn't want to see Brenda yet. I didn't even call her. It was Wednesday. She would be watching her hospital program on the television. That was my justification. She didn't need me when she was with the doctors. She ate food out of cartons close to the screen and gave the medical staff advice on their relationships. They listened to her in ways that I couldn't.

Schlitzy's was quiet. It was so lovingly dark and quiet. I felt safer in there. Like some bad weather was passing over outside and maybe the weather corresponded with our species being on the brink of something terminable, or maybe it was just bad weather. Either way, I had found a temporary shelter, and the storm could do whatever it wanted, because I was warm and safe and could smell animal knuckles melting into sauerkraut.

Just a few seats to my left, a refined and lengthy woman, with the grace of a swan, glided into a seat on the other side of the table. It was as if she had fallen out of a foreign film. She was clothed in black, the cheekbones of her young face might have won a blue ribbon at a state fair—unless the judges were corrupt or blind—and she had the most elegantly silver hair, well ahead of its time, asserting a sophistication, shining around all of us, making clearer what was already clear: that she was not of this place. She was a magnet, and I decided she was French, because the women there, though I have no personal experience to support this, are at their most attractive when doing the simplest things, like reading the newspaper in bed or wiping pastry crumbs off their child's tasteful wool coat. I began to read, or more accurately pretend to read, the TheraRestore brochure, because it was everything I could do not to stare at her with my mouth open like a child who cannot breathe through his nose, except then I realized openly reading a mental-health brochure might give the false impression that I was crazy, so I started to read one of the surveys instead.

Todd Langley, an associate in Quantity Assurance, wrote:

```
I am very happy. I have a family. I have
a sweet car. I have a hot wife and a
```

```
nice gun. I have a daughter who will one
day be hot like her mother. I go to a
great church. And a lot of people would
kill for my job (and my hot wife—ha!).
I am very happy. Who wouldn't be?
```

I read it and then was trying to remember who Todd was. There are those people you don't work with but you work near. I never remember these people's names. I think Todd was the big one who scared me. The one who wore the tight-fitting shirts made out of sports fabric that give a person's chest the smooth plastic contours of a Ken doll. I think he is the one I stood behind once in the cafeteria who served himself an obscene amount of Tater Tots and then ladled Thousand Island dressing over them and then sprinkled some sort of protein powder supplement on top of that.

"I don't think they're making a fortune off of the sausage," the steel-haired woman said to me. This was not expected. I was at a loss. The one constant of Schlitzy's is that interaction is never a probability. It was a temple for people like myself, who didn't want to talk, who wanted to eat and drink and maybe sit under one of the few lights to read a book, or in my case surveys, without any risk of conversation.

"You probably like that," she continued, undeterred by my silence.

I looked past her. A woman in one of the red booths near the unplugged jukebox kept checking herself in her compact. She was wearing a hat with a fake blue flower on it. The hat had fallen out of a different era. So had the woman. She was checking herself like she was preparing for company, but she was always in that booth and there was never any company.

I looked back at my French woman. She smiled. She was patient. She knew I would eventually answer.

I said, "The sausage or that they aren't making a fortune on it?"

"Both."

She was right. I loved the sausage. I actually liked the idea of all the parts I would have no business with in any other context—ears, lips, noses, something called recovered meat, all ground and seasoned with God knows what—encased in something else I don't want to know about, and then boiled in beer. Some people smoke cigarettes, looking death in the face, sucking in tar and 419 other chemical reactions, killing themselves on their terms. I eat sausage.

And she was right about the other part too; I liked that Schlitzy's was only scraping by. It was selfish but true. I liked that there was dust on the tables. I liked that when I had to get up to piss out my two beers, I didn't have to acknowledge another patron. There was never a risk of small talk, and I liked that. Everybody at Schlitzy's knew they were miserable. It was how I imagined heaven. We'll have something to eat and something to read and nobody will bother us. And the beer will come in big glasses.

What had me confused and feeling a little vulnerable was that I was so transparent to this woman. It made me feel simple and obvious. I didn't like that she was in my head. I should warn her: My head is working on some pretty big projects at the moment. And then also, she was trespassing. But she was, as I think I have made quite clear, attractive. Not just attractive in the physical sense, though she was that too, but I found myself drawn to her on some other level, a secret level that only becomes apparent forty years later, when you are in the back of an ambulance and all you have to think about is every single moment of your fading life. If she had been the man with the whiskers like corn silk who drooped and drooled near the front of the restaurant, I'd have given her an evil eye for speaking to me. But he couldn't move that far. He also probably didn't have the lingual coordination, nor the teeth, to make intelligible sounds. And he wasn't pretty. Nor was he French in my imagination. So in her special case, I allowed the talk.

I said, "I suppose it does suit my purposes that Schlitzy's isn't exactly packing them in."

She said, "You want them to subsist," but she said it at the very same time that I said, "I want them to subsist." She was like an echo, if an echo could bounce back in nicer clothing.

She smiled at me as if the coincidence was a good thing. I smiled at her like it freaked me out a little.

A man at the bar was slowly crushing soggy coasters as he stared into space. There was no music in the bar, only the occasional sound of the bartender clinking glasses.

My French woman moved over so that she was directly across from me. "My name is Glenda Fellowes-Allbrecht," she said. "I find you interesting." She had a long, almost extraterrestrial neck.

I said, "None of us are interesting."

"You are to me."

"Interesting has been washed out of us."

That made her coo in delight.

"I wonder if I can borrow you," she said as she put her hands together in a kind of prayer. It wasn't as bad as it sounds. She had nice hands. There were big silver rings on a few of the fingers. Bent and modern.

"I wonder if anyone can be borrowed." I took a bite of mashed potatoes. They had soaked up the juice of the sausage and were delicious. I could feel my arteries wriggle.

She was eating a salad.

"I didn't know they had salads here," I said.

"I brought my own." She showed me the plastic tub she had brought in.

She said, "I'm a conceptual artist."

"I'm unemployed."

"I'm sorry."

"I'm not. It's a leave of absence. But I don't think they want me back." I found some relief in telling her. She seemed interested. I had no idea why she was listening. I didn't think it was necessarily for the right reasons, but it was still nice. "I don't think I want me back either."

"If you are unemployed, why do you have all this work with you?" She was looking at the stack of surveys.

"It's a project."

"What kind of project?"

I decided to tell her. She seemed like she could handle it. I said, "I believe we are all being sucked into a barely detectable cavity. A very slippery sort of crater. And once we realize we are down there, it will be too late."

"Can't we climb out?"

"Our hands and feet don't have that kind of traction, and our hearts and minds will be half asleep."

"We'll be like one of those gangly millipedes who find themselves drowning in a toilet bowl?" she said.

"Except less panicky. If the millipede can be lethargic and defeated, then yes." I clarified her analogy as if I was only mildly impressed, but in truth I loved what she had said. With an analogy like that, I could feel her burrowing into my heart. I didn't know if the burrowing was like a kitten cuddling up to its mother or if it was like a chigger depositing its larvae beneath the skin of my ankles. It certainly felt like it could stick. Like most things, the feeling confused me. I wanted to walk away. I also wanted to elope, forgetting for the moment that I was already married. I wanted to propose a suicide pact. We could make love in a station wagon, parked in a garage with the engine running, and let the deathly exhaust slowly wash away all of the suffering; leave it for the living to contend with. I wanted to order another beer.

"So what do these"—she was looking at the surveys— "have to do with the toilet bowl?"

"Field data."

"Can I take a look?"

"Only if you are willing to fill one out in return."

I gave her one, and a pen, and then left her to it while I went to take a piss.

Above the urinal someone had drawn a smiling cock and balls with legs walking over nippled mountains. I thought we should have a name for these beasts. They were like those Greek man-horse people. Next to the strolling genitals someone else had written, "Hard drives cleansed, affordable prices! E-mail: porneraser@zipmail.com." Closer to the top of the urinal there was a sticker that said, "Sex-Moms for Hire: 567-878-9878." I took out a pen and wrote next to it: "Feeling like all paths lead down? Report your sorrow while you are still aware that you might care." And then I put my e-mail address next to it.

On the way back to Ms. Fellowes-Allbrecht, I ordered a beer for myself and a manhattan for her. The bartender slid the drinks across to me without speaking.

Glenda was still working on the survey. I sipped on my beer and watched. Her brow concentrated into a series of ripples. A strand of silvery hair kept falling down into her eyes, and she would lead it back behind her ear with the hand that wasn't writing. And then a little later it would fall again and she would correct it all over, but never looking up from the survey. I liked that she was taking it seriously.

She looked up and smiled and slid the survey over to me across the table. "Go ahead. You can read it in front of me," she said.

NAME: GLENDA FELLOWES-ALLBRECHT

Are you single?

We are all single.

Are you having an affair?

We are all having an affair.

Why are you so sad?

Because sad is beautiful.

When was the last time you felt happy?

I feel happy right now.

Was it a true, pure happy or a relative happy?

It was temporal. It had to do with an idea. Finding a subject for my project. You. You will be perfect for my conceptual art piece. I came in here because I knew I would find somebody. I wanted that disconsolate posture in your face and shoulders as soon as I spotted it. It couldn't be the woman in the corner who is waiting for somebody who died forty years ago, and it couldn't be that man at the bar who is drinking because he is trying not to gamble, and it couldn't be that bartender, because part of his sad appearance is intentionally ironic. You are the one.

I looked up at her for a moment. She smiled at me and bit into a radish. I gulped.

Are you who you want to be?

> I am whoever I want to be whenever I want
> to be.

Would you prefer to be someone else?

> When I do, I will be.

**Are you similar to the "you" you thought
you would become when as a child you
imagined your future self?**

> I never felt like a child. Even when it
> was ponies instead of horses.

Is today worse than yesterday?

> There is no difference. But tomorrow
> should be pretty good, because you are
> going to help me with my project.

I looked up again. Another smile. I got scared and
looked back down at the survey.

**If you were a day of the week, would you
be Monday or Wednesday?**

> I would be October.

**What does it feel like to get out of bed
in the morning?**

> It feels like a different category of dream.
> One where balance becomes a little more
> important and smells are much stronger.

**Do you realize you have on average
another 11,000 to 18,250 mornings of
looking in the mirror and wondering if
people will find you attractive?**

That's only if you count forward. But for
what it is worth, I think you find me
attractive, and I don't mind that you do.
I am flattered, even. You have a funny bald
spot on the back of your head, and I think
it evokes a certain kind of worn-down
innocence; it makes you sympathetic, which
I think is attractive, as well as perfect
for my project.

I put my hand on my head to feel the bald spot, but
then realized what I was doing, and that she would realize
which question I was reading, which even though we both
knew I had read it, I did not want to acknowledge, because
I did not know how to acknowledge it. I was scared, and
excited. I was aware that my pulse was picking up.

**Do you think people will remember you
after you die?**

I think I'll die after people remember me.

For how long after you die?

[1/(year of death — year of birth)] x
{[number of friends + press clippings +
photos + (size of gravestone x popularity
of cemeteries) + honorary bench at nonprofit
theater] / national attention span}.

Do you believe in God?

I think God is a placeholder for the
anxiety created by unsatisfying answers to
unanswerable questions.

I was feeling something. No one else had taken my survey so seriously. She wasn't promoting a falsely professional and compliant persona, nor was she trying to scold a spouse for trying to carve out a little truth in his life. There was no condescension. There was care and imagination in her responses. A boldness. A triumphant and evolved immunity, perhaps. If I didn't love her, I surely loved her answers. I looked up to see if she was in fact as beautiful as her answers, and she was no longer sitting there. I panicked. I felt a dryness in my throat. I felt a loss. A separation. A desperate willingness to believe in ghosts, if that was what she had been, and the possibility of building a future around a ghost. I lost my appetite. I cut a piece of sausage and put it in my mouth. I pressed down on it slowly with my teeth, so that every bit of the juice would get its moment on my tongue. I tasted nothing. Finally, I turned around and spotted her with her purse on the bar talking to the bartender. She saw me looking at her and she gave a small, reassuring wave. She was as beautiful as her answers.

Do you believe in life after death?

I believe in egg at exact same moment as
chicken.

Do you hear voices?

I think you have a very nice voice. My
project will entail you reading with that
voice. We will perform our piece in a
shopping mall. I want to dress you in an
orange jumpsuit and chain your hands together
behind your back. A woman (me) dressed as a
low-ranking military lackey will hold a
megaphone up to your mouth, and you will be
forced to read letters from children to Santa
Claus through the megaphone. There is a small
chance we could get arrested.

Are you for the chemical elimination of all things painful?

I like the way martinis are shaped.

Do you think we need more sports?

No, but I do like the outfits.

Have you ever fallen in love?

I keep love along my side, instead of
falling into it.
Now, what do you say about participating
in my art project, especially since you
are unemployed?

I looked up and she was there again.
"I paid the bill for us. Would you like to walk me to my
car?"

I nodded. I couldn't really speak. I put all of the surveys in the folder and followed her out of the restaurant. There was a fluid confidence in her stride. The shining hoops that were hanging from her ears swayed in front of me, and something in me swayed too.

Under the towering security lights of the parking lot, I asked her how she could afford to be a conceptual artist.

"My daddy is rich," she said. "I also apply for grants." She went on to confess that her father had started the Anxiety Channel, the lucrative twenty-four-hour cable network that only broadcasts info-specials on fires, disease, and insect invasions. Apparently it appeals to all advertisers.

"People are vulnerable when they are afraid," she said. "They will buy anything, especially insurance."

I found this appalling.

She handed me her card and said, "Will you meet me at the Merchant's Gate Commercial Center tomorrow morning at nine thirty a.m.?" She said it while leaning against a vintage automobile.

I said, "Can I pass out my surveys at the mall?"

She looked troubled. Torn. Like she was doing calculations in her head.

She said, "Would you like to kiss me?"

I said, "That is not fair."

From here I will paraphrase:

She said, "I like your body language."

I said, "I like your nail polish."

She said, "I like your spending patterns."

I said, "I like your lending policies."

She said, "I like your glove compartments."

I said, "I like your hood ornaments."

She pulled on my pockets, forcing me to lean into her. I was close enough to smell that she had never sweat. Never in all of her life.

I let her let me kiss her.

It was a spangled, microscopic world. Entire villages were dancing and roasting pigs on spits. Families gathered around old clanky pianos and sang songs that brought tears to the elders. All the children playing games in all the streets scored goals in a flickering continuum of identical moments. Galaxies gladly collided. There were no tongues. Just four shy, curious lips. It lasted about six seconds.

She said, "I hope I will see you tomorrow," and got in her car.

Do you think people will remember you after you die?

I believe the mortuary will keep my name on file so that they don't accidentally dig me up when they make room for another dead person.

A) and

It must have rained while we were in Schlitzy's. The pavement was darker and the cars were quieter. All the tires went *shhhh*. I had only a vague sense of the road ahead. The streets, the dangling traffic lights, the competing motion of vehicles, the pedestrians I might run over— all were part of a diaphanous curtain hanging in front of my memory. My concentration was on the kiss. The objects in front of my car were merely outlines on tracing paper. The real action was a loop in my head. We kiss we kiss we kiss. Lips touch. Hands clasp. Lips touch. I feel it in my elbows and knees. I am weak and blind and falling into her. I am alive and wanted.

A man at the side of the road was holding cardboard that said, "Too Many Wars. No House. Honest Sandwich Wanted." I slowed and opened the window just enough to push through a dollar, and then kept going.

I replayed the kiss again. It was a mysterious footprint left fresh in mud. I circled and circled it, trying to calculate the size and shape of the animal that had left it in its wake.

I wondered if Ms. Fellowes-Allbrecht would introduce me to her father. Maybe his network could produce an info-special about the sadness. They could hire me, and I would give emotional weather forecasts: "Gusts of ambivalence threaten an otherwise temperate weekend . . . The long days of summer may cause a false and painfully fleeting simulation of euphoria . . . Self-esteem looks to be overshadowed by an unfulfilled searching for forsaken objects."

I took the War of 1812 Bridge back across the bay. The bridge was striking at night, all of its promise glowing, the layers of grime and graffiti kept secret. The water below it was inky. The lights of the bridge were reflected and rippling in the blackness.

Just past the bridge, I merged with the northbound traffic. The river of red taillights curled down to the right and back around to a matching highway below. We followed each other like a string of ants. I thought again of her lips. The two of us leaning against that collectible car. The unpredictability of a stranger's mouth. The heat. The warm desire. The blind trust. The inherent risk. I tried to remember a time when kissing Brenda felt like that, and my mind was an empty expanse. Our kisses had become a form of punctuation.

I almost missed my exit trying to recall the shape of Brenda's lips. She no longer had a mouth. Her eyes were melting away. But then, reflecting again on the illicit kiss outside of Schlitzy's, I felt that fading too. Only a sketch. A secondhand account from someone who knew someone at the scene of the crime. I was losing Glenda's face, the way her eyes looked devilish right before contact, the taste of her mouth. I squinted my mind's eye. I strained. It was all falling away.

A small leaf was trapped under one of my windshield wipers. I turned on the wipers, but it didn't free the leaf. The wipers dragged the leaf back and forth, in arcs that said good-bye, and then good-bye again. It was leaving a party and could never get through the endless round of farewells. I turned the wipers off. The leaf, still pinned to the windshield, said, *You don't want to dress up in an orange suit. You hate Christmas. You hate malls. She isn't safe.*

Stop listening to leaves, I thought.

I was in the final leg of my return commute, along the Birth of America Expressway that defines the western edge of my neighborhood. The Oil'N'Gas Fleximart advertising its perpetual sale on car deodorant. The abandoned warehouse with the broken windows. The decommissioned train depot that could never hold on to a business—not flowers, not donuts, not travel massages. I drove past True Horizons High School. The football bleachers held shiny puddles. A solitary car was in the school's parking lot, its doors open, teenage music thumping. I drove past an Exercise Emporium and a Rebate Galaxy, and then turned into the thicket of suburban housing that makes up our neighborhood. Patterns of houses repeated themselves and eddied into cul-de-sacs. A tricycle sat abandoned at the base of a driveway. A basketball hoop stood netless. A fire hydrant was painted to look like a silver robot. The bushes in front of our house were scruffy orphans. The house looked unplugged and asleep.

The front door was unlocked. All the lights were off except for the imitation stained-glass fixture that hangs above our kitchen table. A note was waiting for me: *You missed another good episode. Dr. Tillory has cancer again. Also, you still haven't read the letter I gave you the other morning. I'm disappointed.*

I sat at the table in the near dark and held my head. It was a bowling ball. Heavy. Holes you wanted to stick your fingers in, opening up a lust to hurl.

I looked around at my home, the familiar items coated in darkness: cupboards, spoons, telephones, bills, coupons affixed to the refrigerator, a cat toy on the floor. I felt entombed. My head, my marriage, my house—all felt unmoored. A clumsy tower of wooden blocks engineered by children. I put the surveys on the table, laid them out in front of me, and belched up sausage and beer. I knew then.

Einstein's theory of relativity says that measuring all the smiles and frowns in a falling elevator will not reveal the speed of the fall. The surveys were useless. We were all plummeting at the exact same rate. I was out of a job and my project was impotent. I found that to be true in a brief moment of clarity that rang through a swelling headache. There was no world to save. There was no me to save it. For half a moment I thought I could go to the mall with Glenda and warn the shoppers through the megaphone. But I knew that all the shoppers and all their hot wives would put on headphones and listen to their own music to protect themselves from the ricochet of meaning. They would look at us like we were Hare Krishnas. Not asking "What is that important message they speak?" but "Why is there bird shit on their foreheads?"

I went upstairs to stare quietly at my sleeping wife. She looked peaceful. She didn't snore, but I could hear her breathing softly. She looked like a baby animal. She looked ready to drool. The television was still on, carving a glow into the darkness and offering her new products for her dreams. I turned it off and left her.

I took six of every type of pill we had in the medicine cabinet and sat on the toilet with the lid down. I had the pills in my hand: round, flat, oval, white, yellow, blue. Dividing lines drawn down the center for responsible dosage. Before each pill I said aloud, "Are you going to stop yourself from taking this pill?" Every time I answered the question by swallowing a pill.

I wrote a two-line poem on a cube of toilet paper. My pocket was still full of pens I'd stolen from the office. The ink bled and expanded into the absorbent tissue, but it was still legible. Two lines were all I could write. There was no note that could explain. The truth, the real truth, is only reduced by explanations. What I wrote down made sense to me, but only because nothing in the world made sense to me. I went back to the bedroom and put the poem under Brenda's pillow. She awoke long enough to say "There's Chinese in the fridge," and then she fell back asleep.

Downstairs I poured myself a glass of Old Grandma to sip on while I waited it out. I was about to sit down in the chair that had belonged to Brenda's dead uncle when I remembered the letter. I was cautious walking from the living room to the kitchen for the letter, and then back to the living room again. I didn't want to shake up the pills in my stomach or get too dizzy. I was careful about my steps.

We had inherited the massive corduroy chair from Brenda's Uncle Henry. Neither of us wanted it, because it was ugly, but Brenda's mother seemed offended, so we took it, and then we soon realized that the ugliness was outweighed by the lazy brilliance of the thing. It was one of the few places I could relax. I sat in it with the letter. I sniffed the envelope. It smelled like nothing. Old paper. My name on the front of it was fading. Black ink that now looked brown.

Dear Ray,

Do not panic. Please, do not panic. I am guessing that it has been about seven years since I wrote this. Since you wrote this. I gave this to Brenda and told her to give it to you the next time you started to seem a little off. It seems to be about every seven years that you need to read one of these. Are you beginning to wonder if the earth's rotation has slowed down? Do you see the faces of your elementary school teachers in the clouds crying down tears on the earth? Perhaps you have started writing to prisoners, or are trying to make the pigeons feel better about themselves. Once you cried when you saw an old house being torn down, and you swore that each plank was a part of you. You felt like your arms were being ripped off and nobody believed you. You are probably going through something like that right now. Slow down. Take a breath. The government can help you. Call this number: 1-888-899-9090. I have to believe people will still be using phones when you read this. You have called the number before. They do something to your skull. It probably doesn't even hurt anymore. It is really not so bad. You lie back on a bed. They tell you to think about anything you want, while you wait for the drugs to kick in. Ideally something restful. Last time I thought about sex, but I think even that is okay. A giant white helmet-shaped thing attached to a small crane swings your way and covers your head. That's about when you fade out, or you may just see pink wavy lines while you hear doctors sharpening things and talking about their plans for the weekend. It feels like your head is a stringed instrument and they are twisting the tuning pegs to correct the intonation, except tuning it involves microscopic needles in your brain. And then you rest. They have a television above the bed that you can watch, and it plays encouraging life-affirming programming while you settle down from the electrical charges and the sounds of spinning blades. Some of the programs are pretty good. Then they recommend that you write yourself a letter because often the initial memory of the event quickly fades away, which is probably for the best. But maybe things have changed. Anyway, don't give up. Ask for a little help. It is out there. You will resist because you don't want to ask for help. Usually you feel like you are the only one who can tell what's going on with you. But it's not like that. It's the opposite. Take the help. Take the help. Take care of yourself. If you are reading this, the whole world hurts too much and it is more than you can handle. Call the number.

Love,

Raymond

I started to feel the dull deceleration of the Lortab plus Vicodin plus pentobarbital plus Xanax plus Librium plus Benadryl plus melatonin plus vitamin E. The letter seemed familiar. I thought about calling the number, but then I thought about Switzerland. When I graduated from college my mother surprised me and gave me money to travel around Europe. I saw churches and wrote postcards and stared at people on trains. Poor planning had me stopping over for a night in a city next to a river where they made pills for human pains. It was a wide river, but because it was Swiss, it was not wild. Or maybe it was well-behaved because it was fed a cocktail of pharmaceutical waste. I was feeling well-behaved myself, lying back in Uncle Henry's chair. I was seeing a river of pills. The chair was a rowboat, and I was dipping the oars into capsules and tablets, and hearing the echoes of men and women in lab coats hammering out powders.

I thought again about calling the number. I couldn't imagine locating the energy to get up and find the telephone. I was a little thirsty. My head ticked slower. It was looking for a finish line. I wondered if Brenda would remarry. It wasn't nice what I was doing. I wasn't helping things. I looked to the side of the chair, down at the floor. I could see through the rug, through the floorboards, deep into the core of the earth. A small, hairless man with moon-colored skin was operating furnaces that powered our collective reality. He was shoveling coal into ovens, sweating and smiling. He looked up and waved at me.

I said, *Does this matter? Does one person matter? Is it rude to make your wife disengage your dead body from the recliner and take it to the morgue?*

And he said, *Morgues offer pickup services, and it doesn't matter all that much when you go.* He said, *You probably overreacted, but there is nothing about your mind or soul that is indispensable. And besides, I don't know you that well, but my guess is you would find the future pretty disappointing.*

My mouth was chalky. I kept telling myself to go get a glass of water. And then I would wait to see if I got up to get the water, and would find that I was still in the chair. My self wasn't listening to myself. My self was too busy watching my self's eyelids failing to resist their growing weight. With every ounce of energy I could gather, I reached for the remote control on the table next to the chair, and I clicked on the TV. I thought this might help me confirm that I was still experiencing the living world. What I found was that everybody on every channel was selling knives.

I closed my eyes. I said, *You are only going to close your eyes for a second, but you won't keep them closed, because maybe you don't want to slip away.*

I saw silver static. I saw diagonal lines descending a staircase. I opened my eyes and I could see back through the living room and on through the kitchen and around the corner into the front hallway. A man was by the front door. He was wearing a sweatshirt with my name on it, but in foreign letters. He was trying to turn the doorknob as quietly as possible so that nobody could hear him slink off.

Do you believe in life after death?

No, unless that is what I am experiencing at the moment. I believe, or at least hope for, complete memory loss after death. I believe in getting drunk after death and sleeping with a lot of dead people who also just died and can't believe their luck and are temporarily relieved that they no longer have to pay taxes, even though soon enough they will realize they do kind of miss paying taxes and having aches in their bones and a hunger to fill and feeling like some larger force, like the cable company, has power over them.

A rainstorm had passed through while we were in Schlitzy's and left behind fifteen minutes of cool. The roads were wet, the dirt was hidden in the moisture, the cars were hushing each other.

I wondered if I could freeze my mind in one moment. Press pause. Blow it up like a photo. Highlight the titillating parts. Capture the kiss and me in it in a big block of ice.

A yellow leaf, curled on the edges, was trapped under a wiper. Pinned down like a driver after a crash. It said to me: *Help.* Then it said, *You have a heart. Use it. Enjoy the blood surging through you. I'm tired of your excuses.* I set the windshield wipers in motion, but the leaf wouldn't budge. The rain had him glued to the glass. The leaf said, *Go home. You have a home. You have a lovely wife. You are not a performance artist.*

When the traffic is light I like to take the War of 1812 Bridge going back across the bay. Brenda and I had ridden across it on our bicycles once, when that was still legal. I felt

a certain loyalty to the structure. The taillights at night arc-
ing over the span were beautiful despite themselves, despite the stupid drivers and their stupid, bloated vehicles.

I thought about Glenda and her project. I thought
about her father. His resources. I wondered if he might
fund my research or give me my own channel. "*Your Fallen
Hopes*, with your host, Raymond Champs, emotional
downgrader to the stars."

I was in the final stretch of my return commute. A Jap-
anese restaurant had taken over the Italian restaurant that
had taken over the natural foods store. The Storage Time
on East 423rd was offering a special on packing tape. The
high school where Brenda had learned self-defense after
work looked wet and forgotten. A junker was sitting in the
parking lot with its doors open and adolescent beats pouring out in a plea for attention.

I drove past a Garden Mania and a Waterfall of Toys
and turned into our subdivision. The landscape went from
commercial sprawl to the repetition of five different home
designs in semirandom formations. Brown neo-Tudor,
green ranch, white Sears Roebuck. Shingle, wood, aluminum, stucco. Mailbox, sprinkler, old car, rubber trash can.

Brenda had left a note on the kitchen table, waiting for
me under the spotlight of our imitation Tiffany chandelier.
*Nurse Blaatz performed a surgical operation on Nurse Van Cleef
when nobody was looking. Your loss. It was awesome. Also, read
the fucking letter I left out for you. I gave it to you two days ago.
Stop being rude and read it.*

I looked around. It was dark. Domestic items united in

undefined shadows. The digital clock on the microwave looked extra green. As bad as my job had been, I did not find relief when I realized I would now be spending my days around this kitchen, in this house, choking on reminders of the life I didn't love.

Our lives capture us. They tie our arms behind our backs in insurance payments and greeting cards. The thought of it hurt my head. That's what I wanted to scream, in my most captivating scream, to the people in the shopping mall: We live in a world where we have to pay somebody else to think up something to say on our behalf for our own mother's birthday.

I thought about writing Brenda a note. A confession. *I'm leaving you for a woman who thinks conceptually. I trust that within about a week you'll realize I am doing you a favor. Oh yeah, I more or less lost my job.*

Instead I grabbed the letter and took it to the La-Z-Boy we had inherited against our wishes. I kicked up my feet and opened the letter. The paper felt old. My handwriting was better then than it is now. I must be slipping, or I must have cared. It was folded neatly in thirds. It said:

Dear Ray,

   I don't want you to forget this moment. The surge in your heart. The way the air feels in your lungs. The way your feet are alive. Every second of your life feels like putting on new socks over clean feet. Is

that a corny thing to say? Maybe it is. That's the way
it feels. The world feels corny in only the best possible way. You are going to get married. You are excited. I want you to remember this. Brenda just left the
apartment to go back to hers. You asked her to marry
you. You surprised her. You wrote your proposal out
of travel Scrabble pieces that you glued to a drawing of your heart. On the heart you drew little scars
that were stitched with Brenda's kisses. I have to say
it was a pretty impressive feat to make it clear that
the stitches were made of her kisses. And yet it was
the only possible interpretation. You nailed it and it
floored her. You should quit studying sociology and
go to art school or just quit altogether. You really are
pretty good. But back to the point, you hid the drawing of your heart in a small tube that you hid in a pie
that you served her. It was risky and didn't go well
at first. She said, "Why the fuck is this tube in my
pie?" But then she opened it and unrolled it and saw
the heart. And it all clicked. And she started to tear
up a little. And she was radiant. The most beautiful
face. The most delicate eyes, looking at you, wanting
to take you in, to make you hers, to take care of you
when you are an old, doddering man and she is an
old, doddering woman. They were beams of golden
light, and they bathed you all over. You had felt so
completely vulnerable and exposed. And she adopt-
ed you with those eyes, with her smile, with a hug
that reached the marrow in your bones. Honestly, up

until the proposal, you were beginning to wonder if she was going to leave you for Johnny Saunders. No hard evidence. Just a hunch. And so you laid it all on the line because you love her. Because you are not everybody's first choice and you are a little round at the hips and sometimes you complain too much and it has taken you a while to figure out how to satisfy her in bed, and you don't have Johnny Saunders's looks or knowledge of European history, and yet despite all of that she loves you. You frequently say something slightly stupid and most people would laugh right at you, but Brenda grabs you and kisses you and loves you all the more, and you think to yourself, *Thank God for this. It can rain now. It can storm. The snow may come and trap us. The droughts may come. I can lose my legs. I may never eat again. The world may hate me. But I have this love.* And so, you are writing all of this because you don't want to ever forget how it feels. You are going to give it to Brenda and tell her to give it to you if things ever start to feel like they are slipping.

Love,

Raymond

I checked in. She was in bed. Asleep. The television was glowing the room blue. I turned it off and went to brush my teeth.

I sat on the toilet seat. I cried. There was no cause and

effect. A boy, afraid, listening to his guts, unsure about his
role in all of the wounds, wondering what had hit him,
what he had done, if crime was a choice or a force that
takes hold of people and makes them injure their own pos-
sibilities. Despite the letter, I wanted to die. I felt weak, like
evolution was trying to tell me some bad news in the nicest
possible way. I felt like Gus when the wind comes, like my
missing fourth leg would come in handy right about now.
And then I thought about the letter again. What a sweet
idiot the author was.

I wrote a two-line poem on a cube of toilet paper.
Maybe it wasn't even a poem—just a thought. It seemed
like the truth. I got into bed next to Brenda. She was more
beautiful than when I proposed to her. I put the note under
her pillow. She stirred a little, told me I smelled like sauerkraut, and fell back asleep. I slept too.

The closer I get to death,
the more I like flowers.

Acknowledgments

I have a great family—Porters, Nolds, and McGuires, alike—who have always encouraged me to realize my fullest self, regardless of how unorthodox or impractical that self might be.

The Hunter College MFA program saw me through numerous poorly formed half-ideas and provided the conditioning to plod on. In particular, Peter Carey and Colum McCann put me through the necessary calisthenics and were incredibly generous with their time and advice. Additionally, I must thank all of my fellow students for their patience and brilliant observations.

I have the best agent, Emily Forland, who I could also proudly include in the soon to follow list of friends.

I thank Philip Budnick and Matthew Daddona for placing an ill-advised bet, and seeing it through with great intelligence and insight.

I was fortunate to have writing residencies at Caldera, in Sisters, Oregon, and with the Ucross Foundation in Wyoming. Both allowed me invaluable escapes from distraction. Every day since I have wished I could teleport back for the calm productive focus they generously allowed.

I wish I could thank my grandmother Leah Lee, no longer with us in the narrowest sense, but always present in my heart.

For connecting, reading, and advising I thank Corinna Barsan, David Cashion, Eva Talmadge, and Jeffrey Rotter.

For digital hair wrangling, and ensuring the skin tones of a morning news host, I must thank Tami Gargus.

Every time I am at my most misanthropic, one of my extraordinary friends pops up to prove me wrong. For their particular influence in my creative pursuits, I roll out this long and woefully incomplete list: Justin and Eric White, Paul and Sasha Fine, Daniel Davidson, Tricia Keightley, Bernard Jungle, Paul Benney, Brad Mossman, Julia Jarrett, Carrie Bradley, Tom Galbraith, David and Antonia Belt, Damon Chessé, Karen Davidson, Marsha Champlin, Alice Simsar, Johannah Rodgers, Henry Scotch, Nicole Tierney, mis amigos cuencanos, the Merry Corners, the Friends of Thursday Night poker group, and all of the members of the seminal Bay Area rock band Captain Fatass.

Finally, for rooting for me, and putting up with me, and for being so smart and funny, I thank Shelly Gargus.